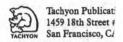
Tachyon Publications
1459 18th Street #
San Francisco, C

Contact: Kasey Lansdale / kasey@tachyonpublications.com

for immediate release

AUDITION FOR THE FOX
MARTIN CAHILL

To survive the challenge of a trickster god, a quick-witted woman rallies her ancestors with cunning subterfuge and outright rebellion.

Nesi is desperate to earn the patronage of one of the Ninety-Nine Pillars of Heaven. Without the protection of a divine animal, she will never be allowed to leave her temple home. But after she fails ninety-six auditions, Nesi makes a risky prayer to T'sidaan, the Fox of Tricks.

In folk tales, the Fox is a loveable prankster. But despite their humor and charm, T'sidaan, and their audition, is no joke. They throw Nesi back in time three hundred years, when her homeland is occupied by the brutal Wolfhounds of Zemin.

Now, Nesi must ally with her besieged people and learn a trickster's guile to snatch a fortress from the disgraced and exiled 100th Pillar: The Wolf of the Hunt.

Martin Cahill has published short fiction in venues including *Fireside*, *Reactor*, *Clarkesworld*, *Lightspeed*, *Beneath Ceaseless Skies*, *Shimmer*, and *Nightmare*. Cahill's stories "The Fifth Horseman" and "Godmeat" were respectively nominated for the Ignyte Award and included in *The Best American Science Fiction & Fantasy 2019*. He was also one of the writers on *Batman: The Blind Cut*. Cahill, who works at Erewhon Books, lives just outside New York City.

Marketing and Publicity

- Promotion targeting reviews and interviews in leading media venues
- Author appearances to include ALA, New York Comic Con, and the World Science Fiction and Fantasy conventions
- Print and digital ARC distribution via Goodreads, NetGalley, and Edelweiss+
- Planned book giveaways to include Goodreads and Storygraph
- Online promotion to include Instagram/book blog tour, cover reveal, launch event, and social media campaigns via X, Instagram, BlueSky, Facebook, and other outlets

Pub date: September 16, 2025 | 192pp
5 x 8 | Rights: W | Fantasy
Trade paperback: $16.95, 978-1-61696-444-3
Digital: $11.95, 978-1-61696-445-0

Tachyon Publications LLC
www.tachyonpublications.com | tachyon@tachyonpublications.com
Distributed to the trade by Baker & Taylor Publisher Services

AUDITION FOR THE FOX
MARTIN CAHILL

AUDITION FOR THE FOX
MARTIN CAHILL

TACHYON - SAN FRANCISCO

Audition for the Fox
Copyright © 2025 by Martin Cahill

This is a work of fiction. All events portrayed in this book are fictitious, and any resemblance to real people or events is purely coincidental. All rights reserved, including the right to reproduce this book or portions thereof in any form without the express permission of the author and the publisher.

Interior and cover design by Elizabeth Story
Author photo by Cosette Carlomusto

Tachyon Publications LLC
1459 18th Street #139
San Francisco, CA 94107
415.285.5615
www.tachyonpublications.com
tachyon@tachyonpublications.com

Series editor: Jacob Weisman
Editor: Jaymee Goh

Print ISBN: 978-1-61696-
Digital ISBN: 978-1-61696-

Printed in the United States by Versa Press, Inc.

First Edition: 2025
9 8 7 6 5 4 3 2 1

For Mom, Dad, Brendan, Mike, and my darling wife, Cosette. You are my Pillars. Thank you so much for loving and supporting me.

-This one's for the goofballs who try their best-
-Keep going-

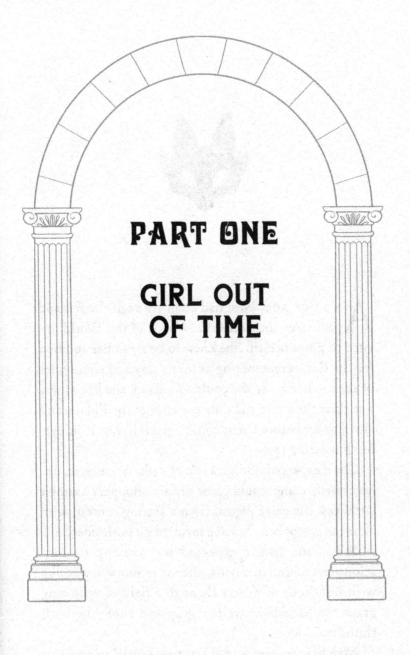

PART ONE

GIRL OUT OF TIME

AN HOUR AGO, Nesi had crept through the red and gold trees that were the Woods of the World, invited to prove herself. She knew to be sly in her audition for the Fox, remembering as many clay and cloud tales of their schemes as she could. T'sidaan, she knew, was a trickster, the first and only trickster of the Pillars, and any slip-up before them could certainly result in eye-teeth meeting eye.

She'd expected riddles, a test of wills. An ancient, unnecessarily complicated game of Grasshopper's Gambit with, yes, the extra pieces. Even a staring contest, with clear but unspoken cheating involved on both sides.

What she hadn't expected was coming to consciousness bound in chains, already in motion, walking with hundreds of others through a field of yellowing grass, the clouds above her gray and rumbling with thunder.

Marching in silence, not trusting herself to speak, it

was a full hour before it came back to her: what she'd gotten herself into, how she'd gotten here, in the past, and the trickster who'd done it.

It came to her in fits and starts, the memories that were a moment ago and still yet to come. Nesi had made her appeal, spilling her heart to a deity she knew for a fact she should not trust and had to try anyway, in that little, homey cabin in the Woods where the Fox had made a den for themself.

And after having done so, she'd been met with an utter silence and stillness reminiscent of the moment before the hunter's pounce, the flash of teeth.

Until.

The Fox of Tricks had taken a sip from a chipped and paisley porcelain teacup with an annoying slurp, put it down amidst a riot of cheap, well-loved paperbacks on a cluttered side table in their otherwise spare den and finally said, "I think I'm going to send you back in time. See what happens."

All they did in response to Nesi's clueless stare was give a mild little shrug of their orange-cream shoulder, like it was nothing at all. And maybe to them, it was.

Then that flash of light, the sudden whisk of clammy autumn air, the mighty lurch in her already queasy stomach as she felt and heard the flutter of a hundred butterflies encircle her . . . Nesi felt like she was a kit being grabbed by the scruff and flung into a darkness she couldn't see the bottom of until she hit, coming to in irons.

Was Nesi truly back in time, here, marching through grasslands both alien and intimately familiar? Who could say? This was the god of trickery after all; their whole thing was making a fool of others. *Had* Nesi regained consciousness a good three hundred years before she'd even had breakfast that morning? There was no way of knowing, not for certain.

Oh, sure. It *felt* real. Most tricks felt real when you had them played on you. You can't fake what you feel. The terror that jolted through her heart, wrists in chains, surrounded by hundreds of others bound in the same way? That felt real. The sweat on her upper lip, forehead, and armpits, her temple robes drenched and dirty, the hunger and fear sitting tandem at the bottom of her belly? Those felt real, too.

The bark of dogs, the sporadic cries of prisoners around her, the flinty gaze of soldiers watching them march as ranges of mountains held them all like an earthen bowl? Real, real, all too real.

But they were a god! They wouldn't just . . . send a twenty-one-year-old girl back in time. And certainly *not* during what seemed like the Zeminis Occupation.

They . . . they wouldn't *really* do that, would they?

A trick, then. Surely.

She tried to keep her breath steady, shoving aside the anxiety attack that was most certainly coming. This wasn't the first time one of the gods had thrust her into a test with little preparation. At least this time, she didn't have to swim for her life or hunt at night with a blindfold on.

Details, details, she thought to herself. The words of Authoritative Ren came to her, his soft, lilting voice usually guiding her through her panic attacks. *Find the details. Ground yourself. Breathe the air and imagine it slows you, cold and fresh.*

The girl in front of her, she decided. Nesi read her like she might read a paper, one article at a time. Her dull, saffron robes were stained brown with old blood, her wrists thick with a half-dozen blue-dyed leather bracelets, the sweep of her dark hair, the shape of her belt, they *did* match a fashion Nesi had seen before. When she was little, before her parents shipped her off to the temple without Granny to stop them, they would take her to the annual Parade for War's End. There, children her age would act out the crescendo of conflicts past, now more theater than education.

This girl's outfit matched what Nesi knew about the time period of the Occupation. And with a shudder of remembrance, even in a parade meant for kids, whoever wrote those skits had not skimped on the blood, terror, or pain.

Nesi's hope that T'sidaan was merely spitting in her coffee had plummeted sharply.

She tried to find a good time to whisper to the girl marching ahead, but it seemed everywhere Nesi looked, she saw tall soldiers in heavy, plated armor. Their heads stayed in constant motion, hands gripped around sword hilts and spear shafts. At either side of the column of marching prisoners, these soldiers would ride on horseback, corralling them like cattle. Many more walked amongst the chained, deliberately snarling their irons together, or slowing someone down long enough for the person in front to have no choice but yank them forward, falling into the gray-brown slush of melted snow and mud.

Nesi saw no pattern to these armored monsters; they simply prowled as wolves among sheep, laughing whenever they pulled a bleat from the frightened. As the two nearest moved toward the outside of the column, Nesi saw her chance and took the risk of speaking.

"Hey, psst!" she whispered to the girl in front of her. When she turned, Nesi thought she looked around her own age. "Hey! Do you know where we are?"

Like Nesi, her arms were in front of her, bound in irons. Her eyes were red and looked raw; she looked like she'd cried all she could and now all that remained was a cold, numb rage. When she spoke, her voice was low, barely more than a whisper; her Oranoyan was lilted, a little archaic. But Nesi could still make out what she said.

"What? We're in the mountains, the Cloudbreakers. Where did they take you? Near Temmaghar or farther south down the slopes? Wolves have been stalking the Telkani for months now, hoping to snare us from the waters."

Nesi's mind was swimming, trying to keep up. Where in all the fragile seas was Temmaghar? It sounded Noyan, some city above the Hare's Longitude where her countrymen grew strong and pale in the frail sunlight and constant snow. Eyes scanning the horizon quickly, she tried to find Cloudbreakers in the textbook of her mind and came up short. Yes, those snow-capped peaks had tops lost to the sky, so the name was accurate enough, but where was a range as massive as this? Some part of her thought she really could be in the deep north for all the snow, in which case she was nowhere near home. But no, she remembered her father said he used to ski on the Dovenyar slopes in the south as a kid, so maybe she was just lost and had to finally admit it.

She kept her voice low, mouth drying rapidly. "Uh, no. I'm not from there. I'm . . . I guess I'm near the capital. By Lake Oryaluthi?"

The girl's eyebrow went up and a shadow passed over her eyes. If Nesi had to guess, it was pity. "The capital, huh? I don't know this lake you're talking about, but if you're from Noyavar, I don't know how you ended up half a continent away, la? But where we're going, you'll be lucky to make it back there in a funeral urn, kyo."

"Oh, by the Pillars—"

The girl shushed her, face going severe. "You must be madder than a drunk scholar! Don't mention the Pillars, you book skimmer!" She looked around, seeing if any of the soldiers nearby had heard. After a moment of silence, she said, "What's your name, so I know what to put on your urn?"

Nesi felt sick. She gave her name in a low keen, eyes darting in every direction. How far could she run in irons? Could she even make it past the guards?

The girl sighed and shook her head. "Well, Nesi. I'm Una. I don't know which dragon of Chaos consigned you here, but my advice? Keep your mouth shut, don't talk about the gods, and pray the Raven comes to you in sleep, because it truly may be the best option where we're going."

Nesi didn't hear Una; her eyes were glued on the destination before them.

A blot on the horizon grew into a massive fortress as they approached. With every step, Nesi could make sense of more and more; for every new thing she understood, she regretted stepping forward to know it.

Walls, tall and thick, made of heavy, treated wood and stone surrounded its perimeter on all sides; the yard within must have been half a mile across. She could see the slopes of tall buildings inside; how many lower buildings were there that she couldn't see? How many people in this march could fit in there? And worse, would more fit after?

At each corner of the high walls, four guard towers stood. It seemed they'd only been here a few months; hasty construction made them look ramshackle next to the long history of this old factory. Within each tower, a soldier stood ready, greatbow at their side. Next to each, a person in robes; a Dawnspeaker maybe? Rare in her time, such arcane workers. Magic that could affect the Foundation was mostly outlawed. But as she was quickly learning, the past was its own beast and mistaking it for a creature she knew could be fatal.

Approaching the imposing walls, Nesi and the prisoners had to weave their way around freshly shorn tree trunks, naked and small, like an army of children left in the snow. Nesi could only imagine what age their rings added up to, and shivered to even contemplate it. Around five hundred feet of the impressive, metal-reinforced door leading in, she saw that the trunks went from neat decapitations to sharp, splintered hack jobs, a guillotine's work to that of a mad butcher. It felt like crossing a symbolic border from Oranoya into ancient

Zemin: neat, orderly, and organized became brutal, broken, and vicious.

Finally, the column began to halt, finding stillness like hesitantly placed green-and-black dominos after a successful grasshopper's gambit, waiting to see what would happen next.

Nesi watched the thick oak doors opening one inch at a time. The steady tick-tick-tick of unseen chains being wound tight danced in her ears, echoing off the sad stumps of felled trees.

It was now Nesi saw just how many soldiers were living in this ramshackle fortress deep in the north. The forty or so that had escorted them seemed to be but a few sheafs of wheat when compared to the staggering field of gray-plated soldiers she counted. Many walked the high walls, relieving those in the towers, while more paced the land outside the fort, keeping watch or escorting other groups of captives, she could only guess from neighboring towns and villages.

As the doors opened, a lone voice cut through the work sounds of soldiers, and the silence of despair. It was masculine and reedy, with a whiff of nasal about it; Nesi had never heard a Zemin accent so thick, the burr of select consonants and elongation of vowels harsh but intriguing in her ears. Her Zemini friends back home in her time barely carried such anymore.

"Welcome to your new home, courtesy of the Lone Emperor of the Hunt and the Wolfhound Ranks of Zemin. Some of you may recognize this fortress as a nascent Oranoyan lumber factory; I can only imagine how many of your stubby little hands held the saws we now operate, sipped your thin soup in the galley, warmed yourselves and gossiped by braziers whose light and heat are now gifts from us. For those whom this rings true, you may be tempted to refer to this place by its old name. I urge you not to, for there is no swifter punishment than the denial of your current reality. If any soldier, wolf or pup, asks you where you are, you will reply thus: Outpost Pakaal, Fourth of the Emperor's Eye. Is that understood?"

The voice did not expect replies, as Nesi felt the column move suddenly, herself pushed and pulled forward in an unpleasant way. Bodies jostled, hers along with them, to escape the cold and seize whatever bastard warmth lay within.

The ground was mostly solid from the cold and though Nesi saw piles of snow here and there, the sharp air of the mountain's heights confided somewhere deep inside her that it had only just become autumn. If she really was in one of the Noyan mountain ranges, even this prelude to winter would be brutal compared to her life at the temple, which sat below the Hare Line like a beauty mark on the Pangolin Cliffside. Her acolyte robes, dirty at the hem now, the neutral gray and white now browned with mud, felt suddenly quite thin.

Entering, Nesi stared in awe at how huge this lumber factory turned fortress was, sitting like a scar on the face of these mountains.

And she was being marched straight into it, shackled, dirty, and terrified.

Nesi started to shiver and not from the cold.

She'd made a mistake. A big one. Truly colossal.

Authoritative Ren was right. The Fox couldn't be trusted. She'd gone into this audition to prove she could be an acolyte of purpose, like she had dozens of times before with other Pillars. But *this* audition? This was a whole new level of horror.

She filed through the huge doorway, shoulder to shoulder with Oranoyan of all kinds, some folk she recognized, others she did not. In her hazy recollection of history, she knew she was somewhere just shy of a century after the Age of Scholarship, when the Provincial Savants opened Oranoya's coastal borders, inviting others to study and be studied in turn. And yes, maybe no one collectively unlocked the secrets of heaven like the Savants hoped, but she knew many had stayed to make a home of the supercontinent.

Nesi did not share the rainscrawl tattoo of the darkskinned woman next to her, a tradition carried from her parent's home of Qaffinu that ran down her right arm in illustrated swirls of water and flowers. Nor did she share the ritual cuttings on the back of the neck of a tall, pale man standing beyond Una, the simple but beautiful death-scarring of Lu'unulei, a shape of wings meant to revere the Raven of Death, who was beloved in his grandparent's cold, wet homeland as the Headless Lover. But she caught the gaze of an auntie with the same browngold skin as her, whose bangles clacked together as the glass marbles embedded within sang, a music familiar to her former tropical lowland nation of Erus.

Her and the auntie held each other's gaze for a moment, and Nesi saw what united them all: gut-deep fear, red and panting.

The voice from before bounced around the massive inner courtyard of the fortress; he spoke like a cow chewed: methodically, unseeing, and uncaring if you heard the awful sound or not.

"You will soon meet one of five officers in this courtyard. They will hand you one towel, one pair of sandals, one work shirt, one set of work pants. They will take you and your other assigned to the barrack you will be sleeping in. Memorize your barrack's name and your bed's number. You will learn further protocol in the days to come. Work is expected of you, a task we know is anathema to your Oranoyan sensibilities. Yet you will rise to the task, for if you do not, we have converted a building into a gaol that is dark and removed, far from light and sound enough for you to reconsider your position. But," the voice said, stopping next to five tall, armored soldiers that waited in the middle of the courtyard, "we are not heartless. You shall work for wages, coin to employ for comforts we will happily trade for good work. Good work brings earthly comfort; bad work brings discomfort. An easy enough math, yes? Now, come forward. The processing begins."

The line stopped, alchemizing into a queue; the captured and once-free citizens of Oranoya made their way, step by step, toward misery.

Her heart hammered in her chest, harder, as though making sure she'd really taken note of it and its furious rhythm. Her breath caught, and her vision began to blur at the edges; focusing was difficult, and worsening with every passing moment.

She knew this fortress had a name, the soldiers who

walked in armor had names, history; she knew they had names for the many halls and alcoves, buildings and warehouses, surrounding fields and forest. She tried to ground herself in those facts, that this was real and real things could be understood if you knew their name. But the fright crept in her mind every time she began to calm until she made peace with it; no names would be found here, not in this moment. In nameless horror, all she saw before her was despair and pain, thick, awful smoke from huge bonfires, blades who had known war's vintage taste, men and women far from home who had started to call this place home instead, and loved the way these people cowered in their long, steel shadows.

As she shuffled step by step toward doom, Nesi could only come to one conclusion, a single possible source of hope. She may not be a good acolyte, but Nesi believed in her heart that even when they had their issues with her, any of the Ninety-Nine Pillars, including the Fox, would not and could not let harm come to one of their followers.

So, seeing no other recourse or rescue, Nesi decided to test that theory.

Loudly.

Nesi shouted at the top of her lungs. "Fox! Please help!"

Her voice echoed across the massive, mud-churned courtyard, finding its way into the corners of barracks and the ears of those who already worked in the yard, backs weary, gaze tired. Across stone walls and walkways, her call vibrated through the remaining evergreen trees dotting the landscape, the only other living things for a hundred miles in any direction.

A moment of pure, stunned silence, as even the hammers and cookfires quieted to see what would happen to this misguided young woman, stupid enough to call attention to herself. As all heads turned toward her, Zemin and Oranoyan alike, Nesi could not blame them for their interest. She too would be just as interested to watch someone try and kill themselves like this.

But she was running out of time. So with as much bluster and bravado as she could summon (believing this was the currency tricksters counted like coins on the counter), she said, "Aah! Ha, ha! Okay. Okay! I see now. I do, thank you, truly! Thank you for this chance to witness your power, oh great T'sidaan! I—I get it! I'll come back home now, thank you!"

The moment she invoked the Fox's name, it seemed the world sprang back into motion. Many of the chained began to move away from her, even as others ahead of and behind her tried to silence her.

"Don't invoke the Pillars!" a gray-bearded, dark-skinned man shouted, his rainscrawl a bright line of roses starting at his temple, disappearing behind the neckline. He leaned away and lowered his head, as though already awaiting the blow to come. Another, a younger woman with a shock of red hair and skin paler than hers, threw herself in front of Nesi, teeth bared at the approaching Wolfhounds, her voice shaking as she cried, "Blessed be the Pillars of Heaven, may the Ninety-Nine remain whole, untoppled, unbroken—!"

Neither of them changed what happened next. The man hushing her was displaced with the same brutal speed as the woman shielding her.

Finally, Nesi stood alone.

Before her a different figure emerged from the Wolfhounds, a man twice her size. He wore heavy, gray armor and in his hand, he carried a fearsome glaive. As his other hand reached for her throat, Nesi could only stare at the emblem on his helmet.

Where there should have been a visor to see by, there was nothing, only the snarling visage of a bloody-jawed wolf.

As this colossal man, this ogre, cut off her air, the sharp pain of dying suddenly in her lungs, Nesi realized all of this was no trick.

And if it was, she wasn't laughing.

Moments before and still three hundred years away, Nesi stood in the Temple of the Divine Embrace and not for the first time, had a panic attack about her future.

"You don't need to pick one right now, Nesi."

Authoritative Ren stood behind her, implacable as the rising sun, mood as cool as a summer's blue moon. Moments after her parents had unceremoniously left her on the temple stairs all those years ago, face tear-stained and Granny gone less than a month, a young boy had approached. And even though he was no older than she, he had taken her hand with a kindness and confidence Nesi had not experienced in almost a month. Together, he had led her inside her new home. Later, she found out that he had dedicated himself to a life of teaching as an Authoritative when he was only eight years old.

The gall of some people to know exactly what they wanted to do with their life without struggling for it. Nesi wanted to hate him for it and yet, how could she? He was her only friend. Easier to hate the sun before she hated Authoritative Ren. Besides, he was the only who still believed in her.

For the last decade, he'd guided her within the halls of the Embrace, and one by one, he'd seen her fail ninety-six auditions with ninety-six Pillars.

Boar, Goat, and Bat.

Gecko, Hen, and Whale.

Jaguar, Spider, and Ocelot.

No Pillar of Heaven wanted Nesi as their acolyte.

Chewing on the aggravated skin around her fingernails, Nesi stood in the sprawling prayer den of the Embrace, where stood the ninety-nine idols of the Pillars Everlasting.

Her eyes darted between the dozens of Pillars she had auditioned for in her youth, sloppy and anxious, who had sent her out of their divine domains with nary a whisker-twitch of thought or rumble of constructive criticism. Next were the dozens more who spoke with her after halting first auditions, after she'd winced through half-remembered prayers and hazy understandings of their domains, who'd put a kind paw or flipper or wing to her cheek with a "Don't pray to us, we'll pray to you, my child," as kind a rejection as one could get from a god. And still, there were the twice bakers' dozen for whom she'd made it past the first round, and upon returning for a trial, she'd humiliated herself somehow, in front of not just the Pillar, but also their current acolytes, months and months of practice wasted, all thanks to nerves or fear.

Nesi knew she was a laughingstock. That no one discussed her dismal fortune in front of her only spoke to the rigorous training of the temple, not any sort of compassion. Ninety-six auditions, and all of them a failure? It was its own sort of training, being ridiculed, being lonely. It weathered her heart, digging deeper the well of her own compassion; that if she had the power, she'd make it so that no one ever had to feel the way she felt on those terrible nights of returning from yet another failed trial.

Nesi didn't have many friends, no. But thank the Pillars that she had Authoritative Ren. With a patience reserved for smoothed-over river stones, centuries in their making, he had been in her corner since that fateful eleventh birthday. His sure hand and good humor had helped pick her up, dust her off, and set her back on the path. Well, a path that would lead to a path. A pre-path? Some road that might end in the kind of life and purpose she had always hoped for as a godsblooded. Indeed, she'd grown intoxicated on Grandmother's clay and cloud tales of stalwart dedicants and even some of the Candle Sainted, those dedicants who were so beloved by fellow mortals, they had earned flames lit in their names.

She'd be lucky if she ended up in a footnote of the forlorn, cursed, or dead.

As the evening light began to wane, Authoritative Ren watched with trepidation as she glanced between three Pillars, the final three. There would be no more Pillars after them.

Ghu'Eujo, the Lion of War.

Qwi'linis, the Serpent of Assassination.

T'sidaan, the Fox of Tricks.

"You really don't have to pick one tonight, Nesi," he said, his voice soft, practically pleading. It was the tone taken whenever he was desperate for her to be patient. He kept his hands behind his back, she knew, to resist cleaning his glasses. He only did that when he was anxious, and she could tell it was all he wanted in this moment. But still, he stood, and waited. A good friend, Ren. She could stand to tell him that more often.

Nesi studied the wooden idols of the three Pillars left to audition for. The Lion of War's was massive, an old ironwood stump that had been slashed and carved, painted red and gold, symbolic of the warblooded and pride-marks across the Lycanth plains; it made for a fierce mask of defiance and carnage. The Serpent of Assassination's was a winding jet-black wood, glittering with hints of gold and silver along its night-dark, sinuous design; rumor was the original dedicant who carved it died from a sudden heart attack the night they finished it.

The orange and butter and cream mask of the Fox's caught her eye, seeming to stare back at her, elegant and mysterious yet reeking of cunning and slyness. It was slight, so slight that you may almost miss it, but Nesi thought she caught the glimpse of a grin in the grain of the wood.

Gods, when had her hands started shaking?

"Ren," she said, voice as small as Li'po the Mouse, "what happens if no Pillar accepts me as an acolyte?"

Ren, bless his hearth, did not sigh as he told her for

what seemed the fiftieth time that year. It came up almost every week's end dinner, it seemed.

"If you are found wanting in the eyes of all the Pillars, then you will stay here at the Temple of the Divine Embrace and you will pray, performing works of charity and labor. Then, you can try again for patronage after a few years. The wisdom you glean in your time of study and service will do you well, I promise."

"And if it doesn't? If I keep failing?"

The very lightest of sighs. "Then you will continue to work until you gain a Pillar's approval. Under their watchful eye, you'll have a divine teacher that can truly train you in your godsblooded magic and you will have the freedom to leave the temple, with your Pillar as chaperone. That, or you may decide to follow a path similar to my own: a teacher and guide for others, in which there is no shame. Not everyone is called to be a divine acolyte and you can live a good life as an Authoritative like myself, you know. You will reside at the temple here for your days with generous, guided time out in the world."

"And . . . and if I refuse that?" Ah, she knew this, but the knowledge had to exist outside of her. She had to keep all thought of it free of her skull. Instead, she left it to Ren to crush her dreams of freedom, rather than let that knowledge burn her in its keeping, like an ember too hot to hold.

To his credit, he didn't sigh this time. "If you refuse, if teaching or life as an acolyte is kept from you, then you will be asked to transfer to the Smiling Days Temple deep in the hinterlands of Mount Gethresu. You will have your every need looked after for the rest of your Ravenless days. Everything you ask will be yours."

"Except freedom."

She heard his nod because he did it every time they reached this point in her panic attack. "Except your freedom, yes, Nesi. No godsblooded, no matter how weak the divine spark in their body, may wander the world without patronage, oversight, and yes, guard. We've lost too many to black market alchemists looking for divine supply to work their illegal Dawntongue rituals, or inexperienced youth burning too hot, too bright, from the untrained power inside them. Many were stolen or lost before their time, with no Pillar to actively safeguard or help them. I don't need to remind you of the Stormgold Coast or the constant garrison of Qaffinu Thorns around the Sobbing City."

It hadn't used to be like that, she knew. Centuries and centuries ago, when the world was closer with its Pillars, it had been understood: those with a divine spark in them—be it by blood, blessing, or bona fide chance—were to be protected, not used. But then, she knew, the Tomes of Foundation had been stolen out from under Gren'Hass the Owl. And the Dawntongue made its way into the world.

A language of the Pillars and for them alone, rituals of war, coin, love, luck, and more were crafted and recorded, spreading far before they could be recovered by Saint Studious and Her Knights of Lore. But the kidnapping of divine children only began in earnest after the Agreement of Fundament was signed. Once those god-fueled rituals became illegal, and the blood of willing volunteers stopped flowing, it became even more dangerous for someone like her or Ren to walk the world alone.

Like all godsblooded kids, Nesi knew what she looked like through obsidian glass, knew that even when the power of her great-grandfather was nascent within her, she shined with the dawn light of the Pillars. And like all godsblooded kids, she knew: if she went into the world without patronage, training, or both, there were a lot of corners of the Foundation she would not survive long enough to enjoy.

Damn the power in her blood that tempted alchemist and addict alike, damn those hopeless little demigods of old, glutted on divinity and magic with no brain cells to split between them. Damn her great-grandmother for her loving and tender affair of two years with the Bison of Journeys before he did what he did and wandered afield, but not before leaving her with a little human calf.

Damn herself most of all. Years of auditioning and Nesi had failed out with almost every Pillar that existed, including her own great-fucking-grandfather. She'd never be so haunted as when she stared into the amber-thick-as-honey eyes of a god and truly saw herself in them for the first time. And then to feel the utter embarrassment as he shook his massive, shaggy head, flicked his long tail, and said, "Are you *sure* you're Joni's little one?"

There was something particularly heartrending about hearing a god speak of you in doubt, especially one you were related to.

She turned back to Ren and she didn't care that there were tears in her eyes. He had seen her in so many stages of distress; this was no different. She stared at him, vehement and hurt and wanting so badly to escape to that terrible temple in the mountains while also wishing to burn it down with every ounce of that small divine spark of magic she had.

Silence between them. They each knew their lines by heart at this point, though the act had come to hurt.

He took a step forward, smoothed out the dark beard he was trying to grow, and put a hand on her shoulder. "It's almost sunset. Offerings are about to end for the day. Why don't we go to dinner? I hear its ginger pork night with those little starfruits you like for dessert. C'mon. You don't need to rush this, Nesi. Whoever you end up with, now or ten years from now . . . it's important. Age is no bar to your calling, whenever it comes, whoever it comes from. You'll need time to think it over."

Time. All she wanted was time. Time to live her *own* life. Free of expectation, free of mountain temples with walls as good as any prison cell, free to make meaning of her own! And time like that? Time like that was running thin.

"No," she said, surprised at the iron in her voice. Turning from him, Nesi walked up to the Fox. She grabbed a stick of incense, lit it off the end of a ceremonial candle and put it in the sand at the foot of the wooden pillar. "I don't need to think. I don't need more time when all I'll use it for is panic and anxiety. I'm no soldier. And believe me, I'm no assassin. But you've always said that I'm a pain in the ass, so that leaves only one Pillar for me."

She turned and saw a frown appear on his face. "Nesi . . . no, I don't know if you understand the Fox. I don't think even I understand them! What exactly they do. Who exactly they are. They're not all fun and games, their stories are not always . . . kind. Often, they can be sad, even tragic!"

"What's to know?" she said, her face growing hot as she got to her knees before the Pillar. "They're a lovable fox that tromps through the Woods of the World and plays pranks on their siblings. They owe the Toad ten thousand golden flies, they laughed the Wolf out of the pantheon, and they love watercolor painting. I can get into that. I love making mischief. By the Pillars, I'm positively goofy!" She started moving her hands into prayer-motion, passing them in front of the burning stick of incense.

Ren broke form and took a step forward; Nesi didn't enjoy the sudden scent of perspiration coming off him, but she didn't hate it either. Good. Maybe he should be a little nervous. "Those are just . . . clay and cloud tales, Nesi. Stories we tell little kids to teach them morals. And the Fox isn't always the hero in those, are they? Don't forget that there are older tales and darker morals that the Fox deals in. Bittersweet stories, lessons given and lessons learned that each bruise in different ways. Are you ready for one of *those* to possibly be your story?"

The incense stick began to glow the burnt color of caramel and dead autumn leaves. As Ren continued panicking behind her, it only made Nesi double-down.

If he was so worried, well, then that was exactly the direction she wanted to head in. Maybe that had been her problem this whole time; doing what people expected.

"Right, right, they're a trickster, through and through. I know of the Fox and the Turtle, the Peach Race with the Stallion, the Downfall of the Spider, all of them. I know to stay sharp!" She kept her eyes fixed to that glowing stick, whose burning light began to wobble and waver like a candle flame fighting a breeze. She had to admit, this part would never get old, her own little spark of divinity helping her pull apart reality like spun sugar.

"Nesi!" Ren's voice was a crack of nervous thunder in the evening quiet of the temple. "You're not thinking!"

The wavering light curved, became an orb, became an eye. The eye opened to look at Nesi with an unabashed level of glee and curiosity. A voice like smoking silk slid across her mind like a bow across a violin string.

Well, well, well. Who do we have here?

Outloud, Nesi said, "T'sidaan, Fox of Tricks, my name is Nesi and I've come to audition as your acolyte."

If Ren tried to intervene, it was nothing Nesi could see. All she saw was the glowing golden eye turn sideways, grow sharp little teeth, and turn into a burning bronze smile.

Oh, now this could be so very fun. I haven't had an audition in many moons, child. Come on in then, little acolyte. Let's talk, you and me. Face to face.

In a flash of first-autumn light and with the scent of fresh cinnamon on the air, Nesi disappeared with a smile, thinking she had finally found the right Pillar for her.

The last thing she saw in her minds-eye was that mountain temple, high and away, a frozen oubliette where the many bastards of the gods would live and die and wither away to nothing but snow and memory, but not her.

She was going to be remembered. Her life was going to be her own. This was her story and she was going to write it, proudly and loudly.

She landed in the Woods of the World, surrounded by brilliant autumn trees, the air rich with the smell of decay and tilled earth and golden grapes.

A short time later, she was three hundred years in the past, unconscious, filthy, and entirely out of her depth.

After her strangulation, Nesi came to in an empty jail cell, her only light the lambent glow of two butterscotch eyes gleaming at her from a shadowed corner. A slight bark of laughter wound its way through the cold dark.

Nesi's throat ached; she felt the ghost of hands around it still and it made her shiver.

"This is a dirty trick," she said, her voice rasping.

"Is it now?" responded T'sidaan from their hiding spot. "Am I the one who made you shout like a trapped goose upon entering this little fortress? I don't *think* that was me." As they emerged, Nesi got her first good look at the vulpine Pillar who had orchestrated this potentially fatal nonsense.

She had to admit many of the artists and dedicants who'd depicted them over the centuries had gotten it right. Many Pillars appeared to their dedicants in different forms, aspect dictating shape, as changeable as the wind, though many either kept their animal form or assumed a human guise for the ease of their followers. T'sidaan, of course, preferred both and neither.

As they came into the dim light of the cell, Nesi saw they were humanoid in shape, but bestial in appearance. Tall and thin as a reed, they were dressed in a rich robe of purple and gold, patterned in curving, interlocking circles that grew thick and barely looped around others, like the fluff of a fox's tail, chasing it around themself. The robe was tied closed with what looked to be snakeskin, a brilliant shade of teal, each scale catching the light. From out of loose sleeves, long, graceful arms covered with fur, the color of which burned hot and orange in her eyes. Their nails were short, but sharp, meticulously kept with no rings to distract from the shine of each delicate five-pointed movement.

From out of the deep dark of shadow they emerged, and it was only after studying all their details that she could look into their eyes. Mesmerizing, filled to the brim with some mixture of mirth and intellect, Nesi drank in the gaze of someone others may call mad if they only ever glanced and took no time to study. Their ears were high on their head, soft white and orange, twitching in the cold, dead air, their nose wet and black at the end of a snout that gleamed with many teeth, each quite sharp as they peeked under the lip of a being who could only be said to be mildly grinning at all times. The beautiful and deep gold, opalescent gaze combined with the constant, toothsome smile made T'sidaan look exactly like the kind of person who kept an arsenal of amusing, scandalous secrets to themselves, and was most dangerous when deciding which to reveal, in what venue, and with how much extravagance.

Across ninety-six auditions, Nesi had never wanted to punch a god so badly. She found herself grinding her teeth, staring levelly as the trickster crouched before her, part in shadow, part revealed. "Why are you doing this? I never agreed to *this!*"

Their ombre eyes narrowed. The single bark of laughter became a chuckle wearing a cackle's clothes. "You asked for a challenge to prove your worth to me, and I accepted your offer. That's the only sort of contract I partake in, child. You gave up the right to be informed of anything surprising the moment you came to my domain, seeking to become my acolyte, which again, I don't remember making you do. I am a *trickster*, child. I don't hand out pamphlets and inform you of what's to come, nor do I ask your opinion on the challenge to be set before you. Is it my fault you failed out with every other Pillar? Remind me who your other options were, little godsblood."

Nesi grimaced. If this audition was going so poorly, barely begun, she could only dread how fast she'd have failed the trials for war or assassination.

She could almost hear their smile widen as though they heard the thought enter her mind. "That's right. And from what I recall my sea-sister confiding in me, the good whale, J'Zimshra, you can barely keep down a plate of fish, so I doubt you'd have the stomach to gut a man like one. I'd like you to stop pretending that I'm the one who put you in this position, my dear. You don't strike me as the kind of godsblood to place blame on everyone but yourself, so don't start now."

So much for trusting the Whale of the Deep. How many other Pillars had gossiped about her? Nevertheless, the Fox was right, which Nesi hated and told them so. Then, "What is it about trickery that makes you so damned wise?"

A little smile broke free of the dark, canines gleaming silver in an arc of moonlight. "We'll call this our first lesson then, little kit. If you are to trick others, you must be honest with yourself about why you're doing it. Otherwise, tricks fall apart, becoming ineffective and bumbling. Or worse, they become cruel for cruelty's sake. I refuse to let that happen; there are far too many of my siblings who endorse *that* already. Now," they said, leaning forward, golden eyes deepening to brass, "can you figure out why I sent you here to this time, this place? Do you understand your role in this challenge? And before you open your mouth, try to answer as though I actually care about your well-being and not as though I'm representative of everything wrong with your life."

Nesi bit back a venomous comment and she did her best to think. Hard to do when a god was staring at you, but she was used to having gods watch her. She was more used to gods watching her fuck up.

She took a deep breath. She couldn't focus on those failures. She couldn't or she'd drown in shame. Feeling anxiety rise in her like bile, she closed her eyes, and counted with her breath while she thought.

Why *would* the god of tricks send her back in time? If it wasn't for laughs, as they'd just admitted, what was it for? Why here and now of all the eras in her people's history? Why during the Occupation?

"The Zeminis Occupation," she began, eyes closed, "uhm . . . okay, it was like fifty-something years of horror. There were Wolfhound soldiers haunting every other street corner, nascent alchemists worked as mercenaries, and there are still abandoned 'education centers,' scattered throughout the country. My town at least still has one. I was assigned a reading of one of their old state-mandated plays about the Emperor of the Hunt and how they even talked about the average Oranoyan was . . . awful. Some truly bitter grounds, you know? From what I learned in the temple, I mean, I just remember the atrocities. The burning of the armada in Monda'lorgu Bay. The massacres at Kijan, Milneer, the whole lower disc of Borahune City. This is all without even getting into the labor camps, which is where I guess we are? Let alone assaults on common folk, the robbing of families and businesses and just . . ."

She let out a shaky breath. By the Pillars, this time period was brutal. And if her being in this cell was any indication, she was not wholly removed from it. With pain ringing her throat, Nesi remembered that she could be affected by all of it.

She could . . . die here, in the past, before she was even born.

The sweet, sly voice of T'sidaan suddenly in her ear, gone from her sight. "And *how* did the Occupation end? Who became the heroes of the Oranoya? Who helped light the fires that would bring low the Emperor of the Hunt?"

Nesi racked her brain, trying to remember her history lessons, but her anxiety and panic kept floating to the surface, eating her thoughts like sharks in the deep. Coupled with the bone deep exhaustion, knowledge eluded her and dread seeped in. "I don't . . . I don't—can't remember, not right now. I'm sorry."

A sympathetic little laugh. "Ah, child, I suppose head trauma will do that."

Then, in an exhalation like mist across a mirror, they spoke, the lightest distaste sitting at the end of each sentence. "Many of my siblings cannot be bothered to oppose our brother-in-exile. We are Pillars; our very existence holds up the heavens. There is no corner of rounded time we cannot see, and so, our attention often wanders. They don't mean to be harmful, my family, and yet. Because my family knows this Occupation will end someday, many will not ensure its ending comes to pass. I have few allies that will come to your aid or mine, so like in the way of most families, let us hope we are lucky, but assume they're all too busy to pay attention to little old us."

Their voice then all at once heavy with history, their words sizzling like acid in the air. "I promise you, it isn't hopeless. And it must be done. The Wolf, patron god of Zemin, must *always* be opposed, and I, the Fox, will always stand against him."

Their lambent gaze fixed Nesi like a blade, and she could not tear herself from that molten stare; there was more there, a story untold. But she brought herself to the present moment as T'sidaan continued to speak. "In about four months, this fortress will be overthrown by its Oranoyan captives. On the day of the Feast of the Wolf in Winter, the denizens of this fortress rise up against their oppressors, throw off the shackles of tyranny, and flood the valley below with revolution. You, Nesi, are going to ensure it happens."

Silence between them in the cell. Nesi's throat hurt worse than ever before. They seemed content to let the quiet command the moment until Nesi cleared her aching throat and said, "M-Me?"

A solemn nod from the trickster. "Oh yes, dear one. This is your challenge; embrace it. Know that you are not alone, not here, nor in the country. Many others hold their rage simmering at the edge of action. All they need is a spark to set it ablaze, a person to lead, and organize. I ask this of you, to use your guile, wit, and gifts to find a way to make history happen."

Dread sat heavy in her stomach. "But it . . . it *will* happen right? It . . . it has to. It's—it's already happened! So how will I—?"

An arched eyebrow, part amusement, mostly mystery. "Has it, Nesi? Oh, but I need to teach you about temporal causality. Hmm, think of it this way," they said, delicately flicking a sharp nail against the bar of the cell, causing the metal to ring. "Think of time as people, think of people as little gold and jade domino tiles, think of every action as a domino falling to hit another domino. Think of the little click-clack of momentum as points on a road in which time flows as a stream. And to stack metaphors, think of me as a seagull who sees a shiny domino piece—you—and in my excitement and my willy-nilly flight pattern, I pick you up and drop you much earlier in that stream. The stream doesn't become irate at my intrusion, it adjusts; your domino doesn't malform at the jostling, it flows into the new current. And as such, other dominos that may not have been affected now anticipate a new click-clack, a new pattern. Hmm?"

Nesi's head swam, dominos and seagulls and whatever temporal causality was threatening to drown her in information both too dense and too inscrutable for her throbbing head. "What?"

The Fox sighed, rubbing the bridge of their snout under their scrunched up eyes; who knew even tricksters could get frustrated. "Never mind that all. What's important to know is that you're here and because you're now here, it means you've always been here. This was already history when you were born, and if we do our job right, it always will have been."

"We?"

Mischief gleamed in their eyes. "You really don't think I'm asking you to cause the *entire* revolution, do you?"

They crouched down, cupping Nesi's chin in a furry hand, warm and sharp. "How you light the wick here is up to you, dear girl. For now, I leave you to your rest. Just don't forget: you're here for a reason, I am near, and most importantly: you are not alone."

With the sound of autumn leaves rustling across the bare stone floor, Nesi was left in the dark, her only companions silence and the smell of lemons and smoke.

A LRIGHT, my little love. Are you ready?
Pajamas on? Check. Kissed Mama and Papa goodnight? Check. Teeth brushed so you don't knock out your grandmother? Check. Check? Hmm, let me smell your mouth. Minty enough, I suppose. Very well.

Story time, then.

Long, long ago, before we were brought forth from clay and cloud, before even the banishing of the dragons and the crisis of constellations, there were the Days of Carving. Many have long believed that our world and all the stars in the sky were pulled from nothing, hands threading ether and magic and life into the beauty we know.

But there has never been nothing, la? The universe was not a bowl to be filled, but a block of stone to be shaped, chipped away to reveal myriad forms. We, like scrimshaw, like the Pillars themselves were carved into existence, pulled away from the stone and revealed by the light of shaped stars.

Whose hands shaped? Which maker made the makers? Ah, ru'lai, this is a story, and stories only answer the questions they're born from. And if my great-granny didn't have those answers, what makes you think your great-granny, will, la?

No, that's a different story.

This? This, dear granddaughter, is a story of the Days of Carving.

And how we came to be.

The first Pillar dreamed themselves awake, so lonely in their fitful rest, so hungry for life, that in their slumber they carved themselves out of the ether. So new was this Pillar, they did not even possess a name nor domain or a want for either. But we would know them to one day be Somni'drøm, the Worm of Dreams, who is still so small and yet whose dreams are so vast and compelling, that all of life came from their hope for more.

And Somni'drøm's dream was mighty indeed. For a time, crawling through a universe unmade, they basked in the light of child stars and the silent space between them, memorizing the aeolian songs of cosmic winds as they swept across infinite horizons.

But soon the Worm began to dream a new dream. To no longer be alone. To have companions, family. Love, or what would come to be known as love. For as we know, being a single worm in the whole of creation is a lonely thing indeed.

Carving from the endless well of life around them, Somni'drøm took their time as haste is not their best quality. And so when sister Ant came into the unmade world, joyful to be alive, she went right to work. As we all know, Fila'rei the Ant of Diligence, is not one to rest on her thorax, not while there was a whole universe to be made.

Before she even began her great work, she and Somni'drøm aided each other to bring brother Beetle into the world with them. Together, with the might of Worm's dream and the fortitude of Ant's diligence, Avro'ka the Beetle of Strength emerged from their carving with excitement.

The first three Pillars, our Little Builders, began the great work of—

I—I . . . okay, well—

Nesi!

How will I get to the part where we came from if you do not let me get to the part where we came from? Hmm? Interrupting your elders, hmph! Don't make me light a candle to your great-grandfather. He has enough on his plate without having to lecture a little girl about manners!

. . . Okay, lei'me. I believe you. And yes, I'll get to the good part.

Let years be the rainfall, the cascade of autumn leaves, the curtain of snow, the bloom of blossoms. Let the years be hundreds and hundreds and hundreds more, felt, seen, tasted but a moment before the next arrives and gone just as fast. For the Days of Carving were many and for each Pillar carved away by those that were carved before, there came another celestial being to hold up the world they had all begun to make together. Watch as Dragonfly and Owl and Hawk take wing on wind yet untampered by gravity. Listen as Whale and Starfish and Puffin swim ocean depths with no bottom, singing their songs in water darker and colder than sorrow. Feel the heat of Salamander and Komodo and Pangolin burrow and dig deep into the earth and ignite a fire there.

The universe was never empty. It only needed beings to shape it, and once shaped, have Pillars to rest upon. An even Hundred Pillars, though that would change, we know. But across the surface of a made world, under stars placed by Bat and Raven and Butterfly, the Pillars felt something was missing. And they asked, *for whom have we made this? Who will all this life belong to?*

And like our Little Builders, the answer came from one of the smallest of the Pillars.

Amidst their cosmic family, Invy'thi the Caterpillar of Stories spoke.

Stories are answers to questions. And so, lives are stories. Already we, each and all, have answered a myriad of questions the universe asked in their silence simply by our existing!

But there are questions we cannot answer. Lives we cannot live, because we were built to answer different questions. We don't have answers to questions of endings and change, of time and age, of death and what comes after, of love and purpose. And if we did, they would differ so greatly from any other being that they may as well be different questions.

At this, they gestured around them at the great potential carved away to make the sky and pulled up to create the earth, the surface of their made planet littered with clay and cloud.

We have the chance to give this world to others. Beings

who will know time and beauty, who will live and tell their own stories of themselves and each other, who will live and love and grow and in their ending return to us and tell us. Tell us their stories! And in their ending, we will tell them ours. Is that not the greatest gift we can give? The chance for others to tell their stories, too?

And so, with clay and cloud, the family of Pillars gathered. And the makers made, by paw and claw, by fang and foot, by snout and tail, by roar and rumble and chitter and screech and song. They built among them the first of us, born from clay and cloud, the detritus of creation given life itself.

Each had a hand in our making but we thank a certain few for their gifts.

On each of our eyes, the Butterfly of Time fluttered, so we might see time pass us by.

On each of our ears, the Dragonfly of Perception lingered, so we might hear and know the world.

On our lips, the Swan of Love kissed, so we might speak sweetness to those who love us and whom we love in turn.

And on our hearts, the Raven of Death alighted, so someday we might lose sight of time, forget the world, and let go of love when she returns to us someday, and bid us come home to the heavens.

Oh yes, many were blessed by other Pillars, which is why some of us are faster than others, smarter, stronger, more deceitful or hateful, or even more joyful. Each of us unique in our making, but for the Four Constants in each of us.

Many, many an age more, each with their titles and

joys and sorrows, many and many an epoch before my mother will fall in love with the Bison of Journeys and have me, and I will have your mother, and she will have you, little, beautiful godsblooded granddaughter.

But never forget, we are made of clay and cloud. We live in a universe built by the hardest working and smallest among us. We are filled with Four Constants that help us make our own story, by our own hands. And—

Oh. Oh, Nesi. I don't know what your story is, or what it could be.

You are godsblooded. I know that that means it will at least be interesting.

But your story? Yours and yours alone? That is for you to decide, my little lei'me'opo. There is a long time between now and your Ravenbound day. You have that gift of time.

Just remember. Life is a story. Stories are answers to questions you learn by living.

What is the question you will try to answer with your life?

Mine? Phaw, children, these days! You are bull-headed, sure as your great-grandfather; asking me every time. If I knew, I'd tell you!

Sleep tight, darling one, more stories tomorrow, yes, yes.

Always more stories tomorrow.

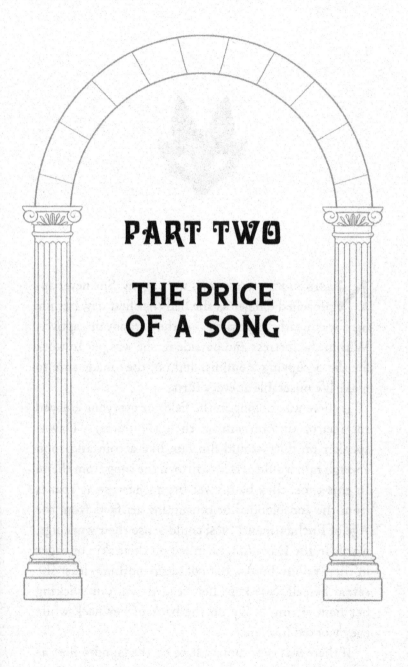

PART TWO

THE PRICE OF A SONG

Nesi's next two weeks were agony. She never approached danger as she had that first day, but life here was nearly impossible for the Oranoyan captives. Within the fortress and outside it, she was put to work for the occupying Zeminis, and oh, they made sure to make life miserable at every turn.

If there was singing in the fields as everyone enjoyed the feel of autumn sun on their shoulders, a Dawnspeaker on duty would flip fate like a coin and soon enough rain would arrive to drown the song from them. In this time, they hadn't yet begun harvesting sparks from the godsblooded or consuming artifacts from the Age of Enchantment; Nesi could sense their workings, words in the Dawntongue inked on their skin or eager in their vellum books, but could say nothing, least she reveal herself. She kept her head down, rain slicking her hair, sitting heavy on the back of her neck while they worked in silence.

If there was easy camaraderie on the laundry line, as

gossip was traded like currency and kids threw suds at one another, all it would take was a plate-armored Wolfhound ripping down a fresh clothesline to ruin their work and silence their conversation, causing children and joy to scatter like wind-tossed leaves.

Even at night, the Zeminis didn't let them sleep without surprise inspections, making the young and old alike stand for hours, exhausted and terrified, before letting them fall back to bed an hour before sunrise and the day's labor ahead.

Nesi kept her head down, hair tied back, and worked in silence, learning the lay of the land as she did so. The fortress had been an old timber factory, a hub for Oranoyan laborers and rangers to bring in felled trees from the valley below and the mountains around them. Much of the machinery had been melted down and turned into extra armor, crude weapons, or roughshod bars for prison cells. Into those former halls of industry, they had dragged hay and thin blankets, building out their makeshift prison. What had been left of the machinery was dangerous and ill-designed, the former workers of the factory toiling to bring them to some semblance of safety, only for soldiers to break them once more and then scream at the laborers to keep working.

Everything flowed from the center courtyard, which was vast and open, but always nearly packed to the brim with Wolfhounds and captives being led from one area to another. Offshoot chambers and towers were occupied by higher-ranking officers and visiting ambassadors, appraising their Emperor's newest acquisition before leaving for other parts of occupied Oranoya. At some point, Nesi learned the names these halls and buildings had been given, the rough, barking tongue of Zemin stamping itself like a sick palimpsest over the Oranoyan names they'd been built with.

And yet, didn't the other captives whisper the true names, remembered in the night, in between beatings and orders and bad sleep? It left Nesi dizzy, balancing this trick of names as she worked. She learned the best pathway to the officer's barracks, once called the Olos Hall and now called Eygletat Den. She memorized the fastest path across the courtyard once called Winras and now was referred to as Komisk, the Yard of Fire. She realized that at every chance, the Zemin were doing their best to not just overwrite the Oranoya, but make it almost like they'd never existed.

Those too old or weak to serve would act as assigned servants to these officers and ambassadors; though they were spared heavy labor, they were not spared the abuse. Nesi noticed most of them bore the brunt of it, suffering from a cruel word or backhand, even more replaceable than any of the laborers. In their silent work, the tapestry of bruises on face and limb spoke volumes for them.

Every morning over thin porridge and sour berries, Nesi worked with Una to get a better grasp on archaic Oranoyan. She had been assigned the same barracks as Nesi on that fateful first day, and when Nesi had returned from the cell she'd been thrown into, she found that Una had saved the bed next to her. "For the absolutely crazy Heron-fuck who didn't seem to get that she was being marched to prison," was her excuse. When pressed, Una shrugged and said in her old way, "Someone bet you had no one to help you, and I said no shit, la, of course she doesn't, so I saved you an extra bed in case they didn't kill you, and if they did, I'd at least have an extra bed, kuyo." And then she winked with a sad smile, and Nesi remembered that whatever terror she was feeling, Una had been feeling it for much longer. If she could try to joke, Nesi could, too.

The language lessons certainly helped Nesi feel more at home. She'd always been a good student, though her new homework in the mornings and evenings was more unlearning certain rounded vowels and modifiers, all the while trying not to accidentally invent those modern turns of phrase she had used every day. And in between the sleep deprivation and the tending of cold earth with frozen knuckles and hands, Nesi welcomed the chance to learn more about Una, when she felt like sharing anyway.

When she did, opening up the way a clam might consider opening, it boiled down to these simple facts: Oldest of four, two sisters she helped get out of town and a brother who volunteered for the town militia, (youngest, of course, she'd said with a bittersweet shake of the head). Una had skill with engines, nimble, quick hands and a mind to match, but her piece of shit uncle insisted she tend house while he tended to the local phengi den, bullying others for free drinks and cheap meals when his loaded dice failed him. "He never bothered figuring out where all his drinking money came from," she said, in an impressive snarl, beating a rug free of dust. "A line of fixed little trinkets, toys, and cart-engines up and down our front lawn, and he thought Kuri'kiro, Rabbit of Fortune had been pissing on him with magic coin!"

Nesi had never met anyone like Una, not at the temple at least. And even if she didn't recognize the town name or the ancient game her uncle seemed to play and lose, she loved how Una told a story with her whole body, physically losing herself in the act of it all.

As for her past (future), Nesi had the good sense to stay mum. She was vague on details, light on specifics, and gushed broadly. Luckily, after dodging a dozen questions, Una trying to get at those secrets finally gave up after a week and shrugged. "Ah, loon," she said with affection. "Dodge my questions all you want, it changes nothing, la? Your history is yours; you'll tell me if you want. What matters is we're in this together. Just stick close to me, do what the Wolfhounds say, and we might even live long enough to die of old age."

So, Nesi swept. Did laundry. Dug up root vegetables from the hard soil. She polished armor, served food, worked in the fields and tended to fires, pushing herself and her body; all the physical labor made her old hip injury flare up from when she auditioned for Gren'hass, Owl of Wisdom.

Aside from the pain, there was nothing of religion or faith here, at least not the Pillars. There was no public praying or worship, no incense lightings, or Pillar petitions from the community during week's end dinner. That also meant that all of her previous duties as an acolyte vanished at once. She had no idea how much time she had dedicated to the care of the temple until it was suddenly just gone from her day.

Which meant, terrifying as the absence was, she finally had time to think. More than that, she had time to watch and observe. To drink in this chilling chapter of the past and wonder why she was really here. And most of all, how she would ignite a rebellion against these brutal occupiers.

Morning announcements became rote, their chilling pronouncements quiet and calm. While they ate meager oatmeal and drank weak tea, officers would walk among them, and tell them how Zemin was here to save them from themselves. It was these morning pronouncements where Nesi felt a growl in the back of her throat, T'sidaan's disdain and fury for the dedicants of the Wolf leaking through.

"You rely on a gross and bloated pantheon. Your days are spent fortifying your minds while your spirit and body waste away. You are obsessed with yourselves and your arts while the world moves on without you. You shun conflict even as you invite retaliation; it is in the nature of the Oranoya to speak in riddles and half-truths, relentless in your wrongness. You think this makes you clever when you merely show how little you understand. We, of Zemin, cannot tolerate your squandering of resources and time. Oranoya can be better. The story you tell of yourselves are dragon tales and shadow puppets; you think yourselves untouchable and glut yourselves on poetry while the world burns. *Someone* has to help you see the truth! The Emperor of the Hunt has decided to gift the ways of the pack to you; that it is better to run together than apart. We, the Wolfhounds of Zemin, will teach you all you need to know to survive this cruel, cruel world together."

But Zemin's so-called benevolence stopped at sentence's end. From what Nesi could see, the Wolfhounds *were* the cruel force arrayed against them. Not a one displayed the supposed kindness they were there to enact, and as one, it seemed they took pleasure in their cruelty toward their captives. Regardless of rank, every Wolfhound shared the same dour expression, the same curt mannerisms; emotion was hard to read on them, armor or no. But beneath the stoic countenance of many, Nesi saw what gave it away: eyes bright with malicious joy as they indulged in meaningless violence.

As the weeks went on, many became drunk on this cruel amusement. And why not? Zemin enacted the Occupation with a massive standing army, the largest navy on any of the Five Fragile Seas, and an emperor whose every word was borne of their holy Wolf. With a single, bitter god on their side and an emperor who had bristled for too long at the standing of Oranoya in the world, why wouldn't the Wolfhounds enjoy the taste of blood on their muzzles? It was cruel, which was the point. Subjugation would always try to be explained away by those in power as something done for reasons that made sense in their twisted minds. And such excuses come quick to the tyrant's tongue.

At least be honest with yourself, she found herself thinking one night, scrubbing the wooden floor of an officer's barrack. *Just admit you enjoy the crunch of throat under your heel, that you find some scrap of happiness in seeing those you despise bow before you.*

Not that anyone would. Often before beating someone senseless, officers would say things like, "This is for your own damn good," or, "Where would you be without us? Soft and useless, sitting in theaters and bookstores and coffee shops wasting your days!" insulted by a culture who cut their teeth on stanzas, not steel.

Worse, Nesi saw how it affected these people—her people, she had to remember. Yes, she was yet to be born, but these were *still* her people, her culture. Same dry sense of humor, jokes meandering and wry. Same cuts of clothing, with splashes of saffron and turquoise. Same circular ways of conversation, gentle but unyielding arguments back and forth about this point or that.

But these Oranoyan lacked the iron in their spine that Nesi knew her people were celebrated for. Even before the Occupation, Oranoyan stubbornness was a quality known worldwide. Losapai Snowdrinker, Borderlord of the Melancholic Taiga just on the other side of Oranoya's northernmost stretch, had once gone on a famous, furious screed. He'd said, "A child of Oranoya, on a single cup of cold coffee and an hour of restless sleep, if given the proper incentive, can argue for the length and breadth of a sun's passage, stopping only once their opponent has changed their mind or until they physically cannot speak or stand anymore. The most terrifying Oranoyan is not one armed with a blade, but an idea, worse if it has been tempered by belief."

And though he had meant that last line to be scathing, in pure Oranoyan fashion, the country soon adopted it as a national slogan.

More still, Nesi knew from her history books that coming out of the Occupation, the Oranoya had stepped up to the global stage with a fire in their bellies. They'd been through all hundred layers of Chaos and wouldn't let it happen again. They'd been bitten by the Wolfhounds enough to know you couldn't trust a predator, not without successful training. Nesi had grown up on stories of the first Fragile Council, led by Oranoyan survivors who would not let the Zeminis retreat to history's appendix, their crimes forgotten in silence.

She remembered history class after history class at the temple, learning the price Zemin paid for their horrible actions, and the steps Oranoya took as a nation and a culture to never let it happen again, to them or anyone across the world.

But here, three hundred years before her time and years before the Occupation would be ousted, Nesi watched in horror as her people constantly gave in, bowing their heads and begging forgiveness for being lazy Oranoyans, for not being stronger, better, or tougher, like the Wolfhounds said they should be.

Oh, there was resistance, but it was small; resistance had to be small to survive in conditions such as these, she was beginning to understand. A smuggled orange slipped into a sleeve and passed off to a man in chains, headed for solitude after lashing out at an officer. Young children misplacing an officer's whistle in the middle of the night to give their parents and elderly a few more minutes of sleep the following day. Once, Nesi even spied a group of women slip a touch of tuskweed into the teapot of a visiting dignitary; it was said he dictated an entire letter back to the Emperor of the Hunt through his bathroom door, distressed as he was.

Nesi even found ways to give back when she could, adding her own sticks and twigs to that small fire of resistance. Sometimes she ran for supplies, and other times she massaged the feet of the old aunties and uncles who had to be carried back from the sawmills or the fields, saying nothing with words but expressing love with the heel of her hand. And when she was angry, she would swap a shift with another, anyone, who looked like they needed the rest.

Part of her great-grandfather's gift at least; when you had Bison in your veins, you were built a little stronger than most, a little heartier. Nesi never minded hard work, and she realized that if she could lift some burden, she would every time. A few of the kids had noticed her quiet strength, and had started challenging her to arm wrestling contests; so far she had a winning streak eleven kids deep.

But the greater resistance was whenever she could cultivate hope. She could only do so much, but if she whispered their name, T'sidaan was always nearby. They liked to appear to her at sunrise or sunset, those times of day when shadows were long and the light was as tricky as the Fox. If it was quiet, they might walk and talk, T'sidaan eager to learn what she knew. And sometimes when she had asks from her fellow imprisoned, and if they were reasonable, T'sidaan would do what they could.

At one such dawn, Nesi had said, "There is an auntie in there, Madame Chivo. Her Ravenblessed day is today.

She said to me before bed, she'll be older than her mother was when she died. She said, 'I hope I dream of her red bean custards. Oh, Nesi! So soft. So warming. Oh, I hope Somni'drøm lets me taste them one last time.'"

The Fox stared at her, unblinking for a moment.

Then, they turned on their heel in the deep shadow of the Yard of Fire, and walked to the barracks where Madame Chivo slept. From one shadow to another, they changed. In their place, a young Oranoyan person around Nesi's age, wearing a dirty kitchen smock, flour coating their tan forearms.

Nesi followed the Fox as they entered on silent steps, right for Auntie Chivo.

Kneeling beside her cot, T'sidaan reached into thin air over her dreaming head, and from nothing, pulled the smallest red bean custard tart, appearing as though plucked right from the dream. The filling was a deep burgundy, and the pastry shell was gleaming and golden brown; Nesi's mouth watered.

From their smock, a napkin, upon which the custard tart rested on the tiny table next to her cot. Leaning in, they whispered in her ear. "I hear it is a special day, Alaya Chivo. I am no humble worm, and I hope you'll pardon a trickster's paws pulling a sweet from your dream to celebrate you. May my sister's talons take their time in perching, and when she arrives, may she bring stories of your mother in her time returned to clay and cloud."

The Fox kissed her brow and vanished as Auntie Chivo began to awake.

When she glanced down at the tart, drawn to it by

the sheer smell, she screamed, bursting into tears, waking the entire room.

That little miracle lifted spirits for almost two weeks, and Auntie Chivo lit tiny candles at night to the Worm of Dreams, others following her example.

When Nesi asked if it bothered the Fox, they laughed and shook their head. "A lesson for you, Nesi. When small comforts arrive in times of sorrow, no one complains of the size of it. And when such small comforts move people into the motions of hope and care, those are what matter, not candles lit in my name. Besides, my eldest sibling works hard with little appreciation. A few candles are the least I can send their way."

As the mountain found autumn's later season settling into its crags and valleys, its bowing trees and freezing streams, Nesi found that hope was the only fire remaining for her and the others to warm themselves by.

But not everything was a Fox-given miracle nor were they favors done by a young woman with a little Bison in her blood.

What gave Nesi, and by extension T'sidaan, the most hope was seeing all the little ways in which the Pillars were kept alive even here, in the shadow of the Wolf. The only token of worship she ever saw from Wolfhounds was a fang hanging around their neck on a chain. Barbaric, she thought. But when she saw a group of Oranoyan passing out fangs between them while Wolfhounds watched, smiling with derision, Nesi had to admit confusion.

It was the Fox that asked her to watch those Oranoyan, to see what happened next.

She caught glimpses of those fangs on chains throughout the next week and her heart swelled to recognize what each had done in the dark of night. To any passing Wolfhound, a tooth was a tooth, and they'd laugh to watch how quickly an Oranoyan's allegiance changed.

But Nesi was a temple student. She knew her Pillars. She knew the difference between a wolf's fang and a mouse's tooth, a cheetah's markings and tiger's stripes. Little by little, she saw: even amongst wolves, the Pillars lived on. In the comfort of dark, the Wolf's symbol had been secretly whittled and shaped and painted into icons of his siblings, held close to the chests of their poor, beaten faithful. She even saw a fox's canine once and smiled.

And while any resistance was good, Nesi saw that it was not enough. Until something major happened, it would only help her people survive, but no more. Day by day, brutalized and hurt for asking even basic compassion, she watched these captive Oranoyan succumb to the story being told about them by the Wolfhounds.

It broke her heart.

Which was why, three weeks after arriving, she sang a song.

She didn't know any songs from this time period, not by heart, so she sang one from her day and age. It was practically an accident.

They were outside, digging trenches for no reason than to keep their hands occupied, their spirits low. It was the rhythm of the shovels she realized later, in pain. It had been the one-two-breathe-one-two-throw of shovels striking the earth with orchestral precision. It had the beat of a song she'd heard centuries from now; she'd begun to sing under her breath without realizing.

> How do you kill a wolfhound?
> Let me count the ways.
> Burn with torch, pierce with steel
> Then toss them in the bay
>
> Oh, toss them, toss them!
> Oh, toss them in the bay.
> Will they sink or will they swim?
> That's not for us to say.
>
> Our only job, when it comes to wolves
> Is to stop their beating hearts.
> How to do it, you may ask?
> Child, let me count the ways.

An interesting moment of chicken-and-egg, she realized, as she sang and the others around her caught on, passing lyrics down the line like sweets smuggled into a classroom. Had Nesi just *invented* this song in this time period? Or had she planted the seed for it to be invented later, for her to then learn as a child? (T'sidaan would later explain the ins and outs of something called a Bootstrap Paradox, then chuckle about how delicious they were on the palate, like cold flame and shadowed starlight, scrumptious in the ways that only impossibilities could be.)

The song was commonplace in her time and for good reason; the Wolfhounds as they'd been known had been gone for ages; they'd become ghosts and cautionary tales in their own country's history. Oranoya was a global power and quick to remind the world of what happened to tyrants. Even the Zeminis of her day and age understood it for what it was: a warning of what happened to the wolves of the wood that hungered with no regard for the world beyond the pines and snow.

But one didn't sing of killing wolfhounds in front of the pack without a reaction.

Those watching the shovel line caught the words of Nesi's song like flies from the air, and she could only imagine they had never heard a song in which they were mocked, threatened, and made to feel small.

And they reacted as tyrants made to feel small did.

It wasn't a fight. Fights had the potential to be fair. This was a wave of violence rising high above Nesi and the others. It crashed down on all of them in a deluge of plated knuckles across skulls, boots digging into ribs, angry shouts in the language of dogs insulted as the Wolfhounds tore into them, these Oranoya who laughed at them, at *them*! Blood watered the soil. Nesi curled in on herself, covering her head as the snap of bone and the percussion of armor on flesh rang all around her, overwhelming.

One of them broke through the crowd, larger than the rest, his armor so bright it was like staring into a silver sun. Nesi felt sick as she recognized that helmet, a hound's maw painted on the steel, red and snarling. He turned, unseeing, to Nesi on the ground. Reared back his fist, expressionless, save for the brutal art staring at her.

In her cell, Nesi's eye throbbed. She knew a bruise was appearing and passed the time wondering what shades of maroon and blue it would wear in daylight. Her skull ached, and whenever she blinked, it protested. Had a bone broken behind the eye? She'd cry, if only it wouldn't hurt her.

She'd been here for hours. With no windows, there was no telling the time. Time was the dark and the dark didn't speak like moonlight could. All it did was smother, especially when starless. When she felt herself nodding off, there was a gentle whisper across her face and the pain began to recede.

Opening her eyes, Nesi was face-to-face with the Fox.

"Ah, child," they said, their copper eyes turned down in sadness, "it seems you paid the price for a song."

Nesi wanted to be mad. Was mad. But not, she found, at the god in front of her. Not much, anyway. T'sidaan was as they were meant to be, a trickster. They only acted according to their nature, and in sending her back here, T'sidaan was testing her, their version of a test. So be it.

But this test *hurt*. If there was any part of her still holding on to some desperate thread that maybe this was a dream, that it would dissolve in a puff of tuskweed and sunshine if she just did the right thing, well . . . her eye told her differently.

She couldn't help but recount the other auditions she'd failed out; in the light of the last few weeks, they seemed almost laughable in their simplicity. J'Zimshra the Whale had challenged her to eat a plate of twelve whole fish, one for each month of the year. T'vorodos the Snail had asked her to sit still for a week of meditation. Akara'han the Rhino had just asked her to read a book for him without falling asleep, for Pillar's sake! How had she ended up here, fighting for a revolution centuries before she'd been born? It didn't feel fair.

And she knew it wasn't. She knew these auditions weren't meant to coddle acolytes or ease them into life with divine patronage. Sure, her failures were simple challenges, but most Pillars had several rounds of auditions. If she hadn't puked, J'Zimshra would have sent her to a lava vent in the Searing Sea. T'vorodos would have made her climb a mountain without lifting her legs once. Akara'han would fight her in a duel. Escalation was a part of the gambit if you got far enough. Through the pain she wondered why T'sidaan believed in tossing acolytes directly into the fire; if there was any escalation from here, Nesi was going to puke again just from the anxiety.

A little part of her was ready to ask to go home, to return and embrace another decade of waiting. But that almost hurt worse than the last two weeks, worse than her tender eye. And by the Pillars, Nesi was Oranoyan; she might fail, but she'd give up entirely when she was dead.

But by the Pillars ... it hurt to keep going. It hurt to be hurt and stand again, knowing the blow would return. There was much pain that awaited her, she knew, if she kept being a shield for those around her.

As the cold of the cell pressed on her, a little voice in her mind said: yes, but think of the greater pain awaiting those defenseless many?

T'sidaan crouched and lay next to her, stroking her cheek with their soft, furred hand. They hummed a nonsense song that could've been any parent singing to any child scattered through time, lonely and crushed in the night. It made the floor seem less hard and the air a little less cold.

Were they trying to be comforting? She decided yes. Tricksters weren't heartless. She knew their stories. Kids heard many clay and cloud tales that emphasized the foolish or the silly, T'sidaan's cunning or craft, their pomp and dramatics. Many didn't know of the others, The Fox and the Stallion, The Fox and the Wasp, when their great magic of trickery and illusion were put to better use than pranks. Authoritative Ren had even remarked one time that often, it seemed, their tricks were born from a heart too huge to weather well the injustices encountered in the world. That's why . . .

A wick caught in Nesi's mind, the idea beginning to brighten her demeanor. "That song I sang," she said, focusing on T'sidaan's eyes, the only lights in the cell, "it made them angry because it made them feel stupid. Right?"

Each eye opened and closed on their own, as if to say, *go on*.

"Where I come from, that song is just . . . silly. A childhood rhyme, leftover to distract kids when they're being cranky, or something to sing when you're on the way to the smoke-mart. Not even the Zeminis are offended anymore, young or old. Because to all of us, it was so long ago. I mean, everyone knows the words, but hardly anyone *thinks* of them while singing. But here, now, that song *means* something. Something powerful. And when they really started listening, it made them angry."

"And why did it make them angry? Why attack you all for a song? It's such a harmless thing, isn't it? At least compared to all they have, their authority, their armor, their blades. Right?" Nesi could tell they were starting to disappear, the gold of their eyes fading like suns setting. She yawned in response, the floor feeling as comfortable as it ever had been. She would only notice the soft, golden grass pushing through the stone floor in the morning, when it would disappear as easily as it grew in the first place.

"Because," she said, her eyes drooping, "bullies hate being laughed at. They don't want to be seen as ridiculous. Could give people ideas. Ideas that . . . y'know . . . could be bad for them."

The right eye faded, then the left. Nesi's bruised eye ceased throbbing and as she began to sleep, only T'sidaan's voice remained in the stillness.

"You're getting close, little kit. Keep going, for many walk with you. Myself among them. And please, keep singing, for you do not sing alone."

Nesi drifted to sleep with determination writing itself across her heart. She was one girl, lost in time. She'd been sent by a trickster god of fickle nature, who was as forthcoming as a sealed clam. She had to help start a revolution? Absurd. Thinking in those terms would only make her flounder. And worrying about all those out there who were supposedly doing the same thing, trying to light their own fuses? Too huge, too much to take in all at once. Start thinking of how small a cog you are and how big the machine is, and nothing will work right.

But helping people? Being there for these other Oranoyan who had lost their story, who needed to see it was possible to resist? Who sang a song today and with melody alone had put fear into their oppressors for the first time?

She could do that. She could help.

It didn't matter if the Wolfhounds took her seriously or not. In fact, let them laugh at her. She was used to being underestimated. She could take it if it meant she could help her people trapped in here with her.

Let them laugh themselves all the way to their doom.

Her sights were set.

Nesi went to sleep and like any good trickster, began to plot.

A TALE BETWEEN PILLARS

THE FOX AND THE SPIDER

WHO FOR A STORY? Who for a tale? You know how this works: give me sound, I give you stories!
Each child claps with all their little hearts.

Applause, like thunder! Hoots like Gren'hass! Drum your feet, wake old, Papa Badger, wake Uncle Beetle, both tired, so tired like all your mamas and papas, your aunties, your uncles. Lucky younglings, you! The world has not made you tired yet. Phaw! What face you make to me now, to Yarnspinner Keef, hmm? Why you turn up your face at me? Just because my face is lined and my hair is gone, you think I'm older than any of you?

Each child laughs in their way, shouting YES!

Never! Age is but number on a paper. Time, the finest wine, nothing more! If you drink it, who say you must swallow?! I have Spring in my bones. I have a song in my heart! If I had neither, would I strength to spin? Nay!

Enough sound, yah-ha! Enough stamping, yah-ha! The time for story is here. And here, in the fire's light, who do my hands make in shadow?

Each child gasps, pointing their little finger at the phantom shape.

Yes! Mother of Spiders, Keeper of the Devoted, Nera'Je, Daughter of Dedication! See her legs, many times many! See her eyes, each a star, each a fire! See each fine hair across her body, sewing needle thin and twice as sharp. Woo-my, Nera'Je is a Pillar beautiful, indeed! And dedicated she, who in the family does she most love?

Each child caws in their way, flapping arms to the side.

Yes! Sister Death! No one more dedicated, no one more devoted than she! And who in the family does she most despise?

Each child puts hands to their heads, making sharp ears.

Yes! Sibling Fox, sibling Tricks! No one more clever, no one more aloof than they! Did the Spider and the Fox get along?

No!

Did they love each other as family does?

Yes!

But would the Spider make a web for the Fox to sleep in if they were tired? Would the Spider spin a tale on a dark night to comfort the Fox? Would she even open a damn door for that tricksy one out of courtesy alone?

No!

Oh, young ones! Do you think the Fox cared a single lick what their sister thought?

No!

Of course not! And hey-now did that make the Spider ornery, as full of mad as a cat in a bath! Nothing angers the rigid like a person who goes with the flow. And so in the days before you and I were brought forth from clay and cloud, the Fox of Tricks ran afoul of the Spider of Dedication. Not by anything they had done, though they had done much. But by the sheer insult of being who they were! Lazy, foolish, boorish, crass, ooh-wee, Nera'Je was in the mood to pick a fight. And what did she do?

A contest! The contest! She makes a contest!

She does! And the Fox, T'sidaan the bold and boisterous, never met any challenge they didn't lick their lips for, 'cause nothing tastes sweeter than winning! So Nera'Je, she says what?

Sit still, Fox, sit still!

Impossible, ain't it?! Impossible for that little scamp of a sibling, whose nose so much as twitches at the thought of mischief. And not just that, what else?

Quiet, Fox, stay quiet!

And no talking either?! Nera'Je, you're a tough sister to say it so. But the Spider is dedicated in all things, even pride! To think she worked hard in a family that loved this lil frustration. To think she worked all day only for Elephant to make music for Fox, dancing under stars to entertain. To think! Always weaving her family together, never thanked, and celebrating the fool that kept trying to cut her strands! So she says, what?

In the woods, your woods, meet me in your woods! Be still and watch me work and do not speak, and when you fail, who more fool than you?

How brave the Fox, how foolish, to accept a challenge with no prize but pride? Even with no fight picked, T'sidaan couldn't let her speak down to them without standing up to her. So they said:

In the woods, my woods, come meet me in my woods! Weave in those treetops high, make your art against the sky, and when you fail, as I know you will, I will laugh so hard and long that I shall cry!

Next dawn, Nera'Je came to T'sidaan's cozy den in the Woods of the World, her many, many hooked feet shushing that floor of autumn leaves. Came she upon her sibling, awake before the sun! Them?! And already their butt sat upon a tree stump. She would not dare ask if that was coffee in the chipped teacup at their side, for even in silence, she knew they'd offer a cup and she would not be cajoled, no way!

In her shadow, dozens of dedicants came with, delighting in their Pillar's challenge, here to cheer her! And who for the Fox?

No one, no one!

Aww, but they'd be alright! For what do we say of the Fox?

The Fox is loved by everyone, because the Fox is for everyone!

And you better believe to this day that boils the blood of Spider and Mole and Gecko and Wolf something fierce! But it's not their story, it's her story, and Nera'Je, ooh, you know she gets to work as soon as that sunlight between worlds rises.

Up and up and up, into and around and through the forever oaks and eternal trees of the Wood Between the World! Up and moving, her many limbs and many eyes moving like a symphony of talent, an orchestra of care, as from her body she pulls her weaving strands and begins to work.

And what is she making?

The downfall of the Fox!

You gotta be one crazy Spider to paint something so vicious in the home of your host, whew! But off she goes, and her dedicants cheer and laugh and point at the Fox, who hasn't even tried to blink, let alone stifle a yawn at the drama of it all!

Pride is a terrible drug, my young friends, and when you're sick on it, you miss all sorts of things.

Things like all your dedicants beginning to slowly close their eyes.

Things like anxiety in your chest, fear in your heart.

Things like the sun moving faster through the sky, even!

Even things like the smallest motion, that turns a set of lips into the teeny tiniest grin.

She wasn't getting it! What had happened? Hours upon hours, Nera'Je moved through the trees fast as wit, fast as thought, weaving and shaping, dedicated in every way. Her sibling hadn't moved a muscle. Just watching, silent, still as stone. But by the dragons below, that must've meant they had something planned! The Fox didn't do as they were told, ever! How were they putting her followers to sleep? How were they making her so nervous? They hadn't even finished their coffee yet!

The sun was just setting when Nera'Je made her fatal mistake. For a Pillar of dedication, she lost her focus. Her many eyes roamed too far, too wildly, her limbs a tangle, her heart racing.

And just as the last of gold faded and the sky of the

wood purpled, when the contest should've been won, instead of a complete weaving to show, Nera'Je tripped.

Tripped, fell, tangled up in her own webs and weaving, bundled up like a lil baby and by a single strand hung from the trees, shrieking. What she say?

A trick, a trick, you tricked me so!

Only when the last of light left, did T'sidaan breathe out. And with their first breath, what did they do?

The children erupt into laughter, hearty and raucous. Even some parents join.

They laughed and laughed and laughed! They laughed till their sides hurt, till they were near ready to cry! Up from the stump and over to their sister, T'sidaan looked up, hands on hips, and shook their foxen head.

Sister mine, sister mine, trapped in your art, you're looking fine! Your people rest on autumn beds, when they should be cutting you down instead. Why wake the weary when they're asleep? Till the morning, I think you'll keep. And the magic of their home, the very woods themselves, held her own webs tight against her.

T'sidaan did not go to rest, but back to their stump, they sat. Fresh coffee continually filled their cup, and all night, they watched their sister cry and scream and shriek her cheeks blue with anger. If pride was money, she was broke by morning, when her cries of sorrow and embarrassment woke her followers. Rushing to free her, Nera'Je sobbed as her dedicants cut her from her own workings.

You did something! You tricked me! You moved, you must have done something!" she screamed. Couldn't accept what you and me know is true: tripping over yourself, proving yourself someone's better, and falling face first into your own problem? Kid, that's all on you.

Off she went, raging still. Old Nera'Je would always treat the Fox with ill intent. No making peace with someone who'll only choose to think bad of you, not even a sister, the Fox knew. When someone tries to bully you into thinking you're less than, you have to stand up for yourself, yeah? And more than that, what's the lesson here, kids?

And every child screams, thinking they know.

Easy, easy now! I'd say you're all right, and the Fox would agree, but I tell you this: no matter how you feel about the Fox, you gotta admit: not taking a trickster seriously sure is the fastest way to learn you should, isn't it?

Now! One more afore we tuck you to bed, and then up with the sun, for we'll be in New Borahune tomorrow, Hare be with us!

—Recorded in ink by Yarnspinner Effis, apprentice to Keef, on the Wilden Road between New Borahune and Lamenyasar

PART THREE

ARMOR FROM LIES

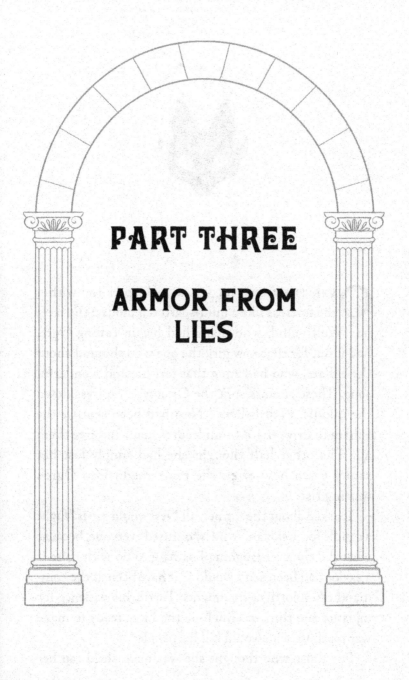

OVER THE NEXT SIX WEEKS, whispers ran within the fortress like a mud-spattered mouse: the faceless Wolfhound, who many had begun calling Ogre, had it out for that new girl, the one who shouted about the Pillars, who had sung that terrible and wonderful song. These rumors split the Oranoyan captives down the middle. Half believed Nesi had been sent by the Pillars to drive the Zemini leaders mad, and free them all. The other half thought she had simply lost her sanity given how often she ran straight into Ogre's waiting fist.

If asked about the former, all Nesi would say is "Light a candle for T'sidaan," which confused everyone, because what did the ever-laughing Fox have to do with this? If a savior had been sent, wouldn't it have been at the command of Golorth'ta the mighty Turtle, his patience for injustice run thin, or Ghu'Eujo the Lion, ready to make war on those who would kill his people?

For those who thought she was mad, she'd tap her

skull and say, "I've got a brain made of water; if it starts leaking out, I'll just drink it back up into my head," which . . . didn't help matters on the insanity front.

But she said such things on purpose. The less people knew, the better. Especially regarding the whole time-travel bit; writer Nelu Jemis wouldn't start writing *Fates of Future Stars* for another century and a half. And frankly, Nesi wasn't invested in proving or disproving anyone's theories. For she had finally devised a plan and explaining it would really prove her madness.

She had to get Ogre to take off his helmet.

Rumor had it that he *never* took it off; even when he ate, he'd either banish his servants from his room and eat in darkness, or he would pass the food up into the slot between the helmet and his chin, the food disappearing with no sound following.

More, Nesi learned that Ogre wasn't just a mystery to the captives, but to his own people as well. Among kin, his armor and helm stayed on, neither words nor breath ever leaving the steel shell. Soldiers believed him to be one of the Wolf's avatars of watchfulness and ferocity. Rumor had it he did not need to see, nor sleep, and that the blessing of the Wolf gave him the preternatural abilities of the perfect hunter.

Officers gossiped that it was one of the Lone Emperor's bastard children sealed up inside the terrible, metallic prison. Serving something called the iron penance, or maybe even making a bid for their father's cold love. A high officer, Captain Vekt, spoke during a dinner where Nesi was serving ale, and his words chilled her. "If it is one of the limping cubs, they better bring back a Pillar's head on a golden plate if they want Daddy to even notice they left the den."

But the Oranoyan captives held a third belief and it was one that outnumbered even the occupiers; there was no one within that metal coffin. Whatever moved the armor, turned its helm, swung its glaive, moved its fist in violent motions towards others until they ceased moving was nothing more than condensed malice, the anger and hunger of the Wolf distilled into an evil that somehow walked in the shape of a man.

Chances were any of them could be true. By the Hundred Hells, Nesi was here, and she was supposed to be born in two hundred and eighty years, give or take, so anything was possible.

Nesi's personal theory? Ogre had an ugly scar, or a goofy mustache, or a particularly weak and pinched chin under that helmet. Regardless if he was a person or a ghost, there was power in the myth and mystery of what Ogre was.

Which is exactly why that helmet had to come off. Myth was good armor, yes, but it was brittle; it didn't take much to shatter it completely.

After the first four times he caught Nesi trying to lift the helm off his head and expose him in public, after the other bruised eye, the broken and then reset leg, the week of solitary confinement, and the nights of starvation, Nesi revised her plan: maybe she could just get a glimpse under the damn thing and stop trying to be so obvious about it all.

On more than one occasion, officers publicly stated there were worse things they could do than kill her, intending to threaten the other prisoners with Nesi as their example.

She'd heard whispers among the Wolfhounds that murder of the captives was discouraged, especially in such a remote fortress as this. It made sense, seeing as how many Oranoyan were being held here and the constant, countless tasks asked of them. But Nesi didn't want to make them reconsider their orders from across the sea, and would not be responsible for another dying for her foolishness.

So it was time for a new tactic.

In the meantime, there was more than one way to resist while figuring out Ogre. And Nesi kept herself busy with a number of gambits she'd perfected to aid her fellow captives..

Buttering up to the Zemini's kitchen staff got her extra bread rolls and little handfuls of chalky, stale candy to sneak out to the children who swept the Yard of Fire; autumn leaves had fallen and faded, and still, they were forced to work.

Shadowing officers to the medica with her head bowed, faking stomach aches and monthly cramps, she smuggled out extra blankets and robes for the elderly, whose shivering had become so severe in the encroaching winter, her nights had become filled with rattling.

Distracting Dawnspeakers at just the right moment, using her great-grandfather's sense of smell to find their expectant magic in the air, tasting it like the drop in atmosphere before rain. She'd burst into song or shout something inappropriate, interrupting and ruining their Dawntongue workings long enough for other captives to get out of the way. It meant Nesi took the brunt of it, a lashing or the burns of a Dawnspeaker's hateful magic feedback enveloping her in searing pain. But the other Oranoyan always tended to her after, grateful for reprieve.

All the while, Nesi gathered names and stories to her like a child picking wildflowers, dozens and dozens in all variety of color and length and snarls. She got to know Oranoyan from the Goldsilt Coast and the Dyfracario lowlands and what would one day become her home, the peaks and valleys of Uloyora, flattened by time's slow hammer enough for the modern capital to be built, beside a lake yet to be created by Moli'vara, the Crane of Mothers.

One by one, the captives of this fortress became known to her, each name learned like adding a symbol to an incantation. One by one, the names of her people became a spell of knowing, of history. It was a small, humble resistance, she knew. But this simple act of restoration, of sharing names and culture and more, became the best shield against the Wolfhounds' attempts to fold them all into their own terrible story.

Their greatest victory, Nesi knew, would be the absolute erasure of Oranoya, the story of their country and themselves sucked like marrow, cracked in the jaws of a petulant warlord and his weak god.

Nesi was doing everything in her power to keep that from happening, Wolf be damned. And it did her heart good, especially in those most difficult moments, to see the other captive Oranoyan doing the same.

T'sidaan continued to visit though by this point, they

often left Nesi to her own devices, listening more than educating. Their own style of teaching, admittedly, was so hands off at times, it was as though they had no hands at all, but T'sidaan would never withhold counsel if it kept Nesi more alive than not.

Most often these bits of counsel sat somewhere in the middle of long, winding stories about this sibling or that whom they had pissed off for, "entirely decent reasons that made sense to me at the time, and so I shall defend my prior decisions to the bitter end." But like most of their stories, the kernels of wisdom were there, and often came at T'sidaan's expense. They still wouldn't finish the story about them and their sister Cono'wola the Gibbon of Dance but would often mumble about the importance of rhythm, timing, and not mixing up the two.

T'sidaan had the grace to disguise themself when visiting with Nesi, either a young page in gray or an Oranoyan child of no particular gender, holding a broom that had seen its fair share of use. They only came in their foxen form when they were alone, or when Nesi was on the fringe of dreaming. Apparently, they and their eldest sibling had a deal about which dreams T'sidaan could go traipsing about in.

When told of her latest gambit, to safely expose and humiliate Ogre, all they had done was grin and said, "Sounds appropriate to me. Monsters prefer the dark; facing the light of day can reveal so much more than an unhandsome face."

And with their approval and advice, Nesi decided it was time to make good on her plot.

In the last month, Una had been promoted to one of the serving people who brought meals to Ogre's tower. Five foot nothing with hair as dark as ink, often making the saffron smocks of the fortress as fashionable as possible, with a stolen earring here and a feather there, Una had proven herself to be bright, whip-smart, and most of all, she didn't test the Wolfhounds; it was no wonder the officers brought her on for this special task. And despite the risk it posed by associating with her, Una still took care of Nesi after she'd gotten on the wrong side of a Wolfhound's fist or needed a laugh.

She was a good friend for a girl thrown back in time to have.

Often, when they spoke, Nesi would see the faint golden lights of T'sidaan's gaze flicker around her. When pressed, T'sidaan said she smelled like mischief and it delighted them to no end, "to find one of mine here among the throng." Nesi asked the god to stop treating her new friend like an offering candle; they would then touch Nesi's nose, say "Boop," and vanish.

She made sure to catch Una's eyes one day while beating rugs and gestured to the alley behind the long cafeteria hall. Palming a cigarette to her, Nesi smiled as Una pulled a match from behind her ear and lit it up. "Any glimpses, then?" she asked.

Una grinned, though her eyes went dark. "Didn't you just finish another week of cut rations, kyo? You're like a little scarecrow in that robe, though even a scarecrow can pad their ass out with some hay." The grin faded as she took a drag. "Nesi, girl, you need to stop. They're going to kill you before you can gain any weight back. And if they don't, the double shifts they've got you on will."

"Would you believe I'm on a mission from one of the Pillars? I'd stop if I could but it's important."

Una rolled her eyes, trying to be indignant and ending up somewhere mournful. "Kyo, I don't care if the Falcon herself dropped you off personally and packed you a fucking lunch, la? You've been losing your damn mind these last few weeks. But," she narrowed her gaze at Nesi, the smoke turning her eyes gray, smooth, and a little unknowable, "if information brings you one step closer to stopping this suicidal crusade . . . I guess I can tell you what I saw."

After a thick drag and a flick of the butt, she said, "So I was on the night shift, tala? And it's late, like, the moon's up and we're clocking out kind of late, when the bell in his chamber begins to chime. I pulled the short end of the straw and went up, put it outside the door, and backed away, head bowed, like we'd been trained. But I couldn't help it. I just wanted to . . . know, same as you. I tucked around the corner, and suja, who do I see? I glimpse a *person*. There really *is* someone in that big suit of armor and he *does* have to take the helmet off to eat."

Raised voices from around a corner and Una looked back, eyebrows high, gaze pleading. "Does that help?"

Relief warred with new problems, but Nesi nodded, letting out a shaky breath. "More than you know, Una. Thank you. It's safe with me." Una turned to leave when Nesi reached out and gripped her arm. "And for information in kind: I heard Vikra talking about you in the showers the other night. Said she thought you were the prettiest maidan this side of a clay and cloud tale."

Her grin returned, and a light rose in her eyes. "Did she? I might just have to confirm this tawdry gossip next time I see her on the laundry line."

"If it helps, I hear she likes flowers. Butterlillies, especially. And didn't I see a little group of them behind the A5 barracks. Pick her a few? I'm sure your smile will be all the buttering you need, but hey, everyone loves a gift."

Una cocked her head, confused. "Those are out of season, girl. Only thing that grows around here is tuskweed. Though," she said with a laugh, "the damn hounds would pull all that shit out of the ground and burn it if they knew what it could do. But . . . I suppose it can't hurt to check, la? I'll admit, the strangest things happen around you, Nesi. The worst being that I don't feel so sick to my stomach when I have even the littlest bit of hope some mornings. Stupid, I know."

Nesi shook her head, the suddenness of the fire in her belly almost startling her as she said, "No! No, it's not stupid, Una. It's never stupid to hope. This is *not* forever. You're going to get out of here. I promise."

Una's smile was small and sad, but at least there was no pity like the first time they'd met. "If you say so. I'll try to believe in you with what little faith they let us have in here."

After Una left, Nesi pressed herself against the wooden walls, breathing deep, trying to let go of the flash of anger, that minor chord of sorrow. As she breathed, the shadows grew solid around her and she heard the fleet, light steps of T'sidaan slipping through fresh tuskweed, appearing beside her.

"Butterlillies? This time of year?" they said with feigned innocence.

"Oh, I figured you could do something about that."

Their eyes glimmered like sunken treasure found. "Truly? The power of a Pillar and you ask me to grow springtime flowers in the coming cold of winter?"

Nesi smiled back, a small part of her thrilled that the god had not exactly said no. "Of course. You're a mischief-maker. What's more mischievous than love? I figured that'd be a fire you'd happily stoke."

A nod of their head, a flash of their eyes, and a satisfied bounce to their gait told Nesi that they'd done as she'd asked. "You are growing wiser, young one. I've only myself to blame, truly. But I can't fault you if you're a good student with a bad teacher. You're becoming attuned to the way trickery can be wielded, I see it. The work I do is useless as the hammer, the knife, the roar. But it shines as the smirk, the whisper, the scissor, the mirror. Those in power often only ever see their opponents as worthy when those opponents wield a power similar to the kind they hold themselves; they don't ever think to look for power in the forms they do not know. It is how I often humble and best both brethren and mortals. From gods to men, trickery levels us all."

Nesi beamed from the inside out as she walked back to her barracks. "Thank you, T'sidaan. You're not as bad a teacher as you claim, though I'm sure my stubbornness hasn't hurt. But I still have much to learn. Especially now. I can't keep throwing myself at the Ogre; one day, he'll tire of me and have me hanged."

They nodded. Then with the tone of a parent educating a child, they continued, their voice low and serious. "Yes. Yes, there's a fine line between stubborn and stupid, cross it and they'll definitely drop you from a rope one of these days. You must use caution, Nesi. You are truly in this time; it's part of the audition. The stakes must be real, and I cannot save you from the consequences of your actions. Listen well: you can't trick someone from beyond the grave. I mean, you can, but I don't advise it. I tell you this as I wish I had told another: survive, above all. Move as I do, through shadow and moon's light, child. Stillness. Silence. Then! Motion, there and gone. Quick and quiet is the only way to elude my sister's dark wings. You are old enough to know fear; may that keep you alive."

Nesi's leg still throbbed from the break and setting. Her face was puffy and tender from the beatings; her stomach had shrunk and mewled for more, always more. She couldn't remember the last time she had a decent night's sleep. She realized that yes, it felt satisfying to torment tyrants, but no satisfaction stayed long enough to soothe the ever-growing pain. "I will. Thank you, T'sidaan. I . . . needed the reminder."

They nodded, their form melting into end-of-autumn mist, as guards came into view. "So, then . . . how will you get close?"

Nesi gave it a think and wondered at next steps; her eyes found the commander's tower, the windows aglow with candlelight in the waning day. It was there and only there that Ogre would exit his metal shell.

"Oh, I've got some ideas."

It took a week more to grease the right palms, make friends with the proper guard, and flirt with the right soldier in order for her plan to be put into motion. But one fine, chilly evening, a bag on her shoulder, Nesi made her way into the showers in the dead of night and transformed.

She put on a pair of worker's pants, bound her chest tight, slipped on some beat-up coveralls, and artfully dabbed grease across her upper lip, in the façade of a mustache. She tied up her long, dark hair into a bun and squashed a wool cap down on her head, with additional smears of grease across her forearms and face, just to add a little texture. You didn't want to overdo it.

Step by step, she built herself into a lie, and then made that lie put on oversized boots. She put weight into the bottom of her feet and squared her hips when she walked, leading with her shoulders. She slouched a little, grumbling about the weather under her breath, even though no one was there to hear her, but that was okay. For a lie this large to work, for it to become a story you're telling the world, it had to live and breathe as though everyone was listening.

With every step, the story that was her armor became real. Grabbing a shoddy ladder under arm, she made her way to the commander's tower, hoping beyond hope that what Una said was true every night after the moon rose.

For tonight, she was going to sneak in and steal herself a helmet.

The scaffolding was there like planned, abandoned

after dark and glowing coldly in the moonlight of almost winter, silver bright and cold. Grumbling about the chill, putting a hand to that "luck-cursed hip of mine," Nesi slowly settled the ladder against the top of the scaffolding, and waited in the shadows.

When clouds drifted across the eager moon, she climbed. Hand over hand, as quietly as possible, she rose to meet the stone lip of a window two hundred feet in the air. Through gossamer thin curtains, she saw light and movement, a man-shaped shadow in relief against a far wall, breathing.

So, he was awake. Interesting.

Well, she would be fast. She remembered the words of T'sidaan. With a quick prayer that the god was watching even now, Nesi hoisted herself over the lip of the window and landed on her feet, hunched, eyes darting around the room.

It came to her in flashes.

Thick, stubby candles half-melted and burning low on a bare, central table. A bed with a thin, blue blanket, twisted and knotted as though a body thrashed in it nightly. A huge sword no better than a beaten, sharp bar of steel, plain and efficient as a sentence. A massive suit of gray armor, dull and smooth like ocean-weathered stones, with a snarling wolf's face on the front.

And a lithe, young man, dressed in threadbare robes, exposing a lean, hungry body, with a dagger pointed at her. His hands shook and Nesi smelled his fear in the air.

His eyes darted from her to the armor. Back to her. Back to the armor. He was pasty-white with burning red hair plastered to his forehead. If he was any older than her, she'd eat her stolen hat.

"P-please," he said, voice thin as his body, malnourished and pale, "please. You shouldn't have come."

His eyes kept flicking over to the suit of armor that loomed above him, a pillar in the room that drew her eye as well. Was the eye of the wolf on the faceplate watching her, too? What was that creaking sound?

She looked between the boy and the armor, saw terrible scars and marks on his body, where the joints of a suit might cinch in on him too tightly, press too deeply. As if the armor crushed him every time he stepped into it.

Or every time it swallowed him.

She took a tentative step forward into the candlelight of the table, taking her hat off and rubbing away the grease from her face, wiping away the lie she had made. The young man's eyes widened.

Again, his eyes went to the armor. "It's you. By the Wolf—"

Nesi saw it this time. One of the knuckle joints of the hollow gauntlet twitched, moving on its own, one of five fingers starting to form a fist. The empty helmet creaked as it searched the room for her.

Uh oh.

The boy leveled the dagger at her, hands trembling. "Leave! Please, I—I can't control it when I'm not in there. Okay, fine, I can't control it, not very well, and if—if you stay, it will eat me again, please—!"

Nesi put her hands up, willing his fear to ease. "Hey, I need you to calm down, okay? I don't think you freaking out at me is going to help. Is there a way we can get that thing to stop moving?"

He audibly gulped, one shoulder going up and then down, dagger shaking harder. "I don't know, I don't know anything about it, it just, it just *does* stuff, it moves on its own, but it needs me, but also, if I feel threatened it just—"

"So maybe don't feel threatened—" She winced hearing herself. Smooth, Nesi.

"Oh, right! Easy. I'll just stop! I'll just act like you being in my room at midnight is as normal as can be!"

Metal screamed on metal as every finger curled in, helmet staring right at her, hips turning in her direction. Nesi's heart raced, sweat beading along her greased forehead. She needed this kid to stop whatever it was he was doing before they both got killed.

"What's your name?"

He screwed his face up. "What?"

"Your name! You have one, right?"

"Of course, I have a name—"

"Well, don't hold out, give it a spill, a spell, tell me what to call you."

He wiped his brow. "Uhm, I'm Teor."

"Teor! Great. Nice to meet you. I'm Nesi, you've punched me in the face before. Water under the bridge. Now, tell me your top twenty favorite flavors of tea. They have tea in Zemin, right?"

A heavy footfall shook the chamber.

"Excuse me? Tea? I don't—"

"Tea! Flavors! Now, please!"

One of the candles blew out. Then another.

"Uhm, midnight berry! Green pearl! What's that one, uh, stone blossom! Peach leaf. I also like pepper-dirt. Red blessing. Silk wind." He took a deep breath, closed his eyes. "I uh, mango dragon is good. I'm partial to ocean crisp. I like chocolate embrace in the winter. I prefer hot tea in the summer, because y'know, it eventually becomes cold tea. I . . . Huh."

As he spoke, his voice grew slower. Softer. Thoughtful.

By mango dragon, the armor had stopped moving. His hands had stopped shaking.

He opened his eyes and took in the tableau. "Wow," Teor said, as he stepped back. Finding a wall at his back, slid down it. He put the dagger on the floor next to him and curled around himself, body still shivering. "Thanks."

"Can I . . . come sit with you? I promise I'm not here to hurt you."

"Okay."

She found a little patch of wall next to Teor and slid down until her butt hit the floor. "How did you do that?" he asked, a little breathless.

Nesi shrugged, clutching the hat in her hand too tightly. "I don't want to brag, but I've had a *lot* of panic attacks in my day. My caretaker at the temple I grew up in, he suggested listing things I liked. And breathing. Sometimes pointing out things in the room, stuff I see or hear or smell. Grounding stuff. It's mostly worked. Good taste, by the way," she said with a smile, "though I'm more of a coffee person."

Teor's smile was weak but sincere. He ran a hand through his thick, red hair, hand slick with sweat. "Yes, burnt bean water. Very cultured. So delicious," he said, the smile melting as he saw he sat in the shadow of the armor.

"Teor," she said, her voice as soft as she could make it, "who are you? What is all this?"

He looked at her and she saw a cloud form in his eyes like a storm growing nearer, dark and foreboding.

"I was born the youngest of my family, the runt of the litter. A son to a minister of war; there are many in Zemin, as there are many types of war that we like to . . . that *they* like to make. I never took to it. He loved it so much that he had earned an epithet, a title gained in the Fengar Campaigns: Grief-Teacher."

He began to pick at his fingernails, not looking at her; Nesi saw how torn and bloody the ends of his hands were.

"I apparently disappointed them all from day one, when I didn't come into the world screaming for blood. Instead, they say I pawed at the air, like I wanted to return to the silence of the womb. It . . . wasn't a good omen." The look in his eye was dark and distant, almost cold. "Ceremony dictated that I be brought before the Lonely Seat of Kehora, the forest capital, like all Zemin children. Babes are set upon the smooth wooden seat of the ancient throne turned shrine. There, the newborn face the heart of the forest, their parents awaiting the bloody howl to signal worth and give them leave to take their children back. In my case, there was . . . nothing. It is a wonder my father even brought me home. Usually people leave children of silence there for the crows and coyotes to pick their teeth with."

Here, Nesi felt the Fox's full attention swivel to Teor's story like a mighty sun, relentless and full of fire.

"Years passed, as they do. Each day my father hoped

I'd prove the Wolf wrong; blasphemous, yes, but better than one of his own proving unworthy. And every day, I refused to fight, to shed blood, the worst injury a papercut on the history and poetry books I devoured. I hungered for knowledge, not battle. Every year, Father threatened to send me abroad, make me serve at Highfort Mogesh as a Borderblade, or man one of the rigs on the Burbling Sea. Mother was always able to shield me until . . ." His voice faded and not knowing why, Nesi took his hand and held it tightly. When he turned to look at her, he had tears in his eyes, and in that silence, he looked grateful to skip the next part of his tale.

"When the Occupation was underway, Father . . . had his chance. He sent me on a ship, under watch from my oldest sister. The last thing he ever said to me was, 'Bring home a sword weary with use, or do not come home.' I think we both understood it was as loving a goodbye as he could muster."

He paused for breath, and Nesi took in for the first time just how small he was, sitting in the shadow of the metallic colossus behind him.

"On our journey, my sister Adera had a handmaiden. Her name was Tsuna, an Oranoyan woman taken from your lands many years earlier. She was miserable, treated worse than I, and I was Zemin. When we spoke, in the late evenings when Wolfhounds slept, she said, 'I'd rather take my chances on the sea than another day with your people, kuyo.'

"And one night, I gave her that chance. Grabbed stores, supplies, and got her into a lifeboat. Because I could. Because she deserved freedom. They didn't even know she was missing until their laundry piled up, the selfish assholes. It didn't take long for my sister to figure out who helped her. In front of the whole crew, she said, 'You've never been a Wolfhound. You're not even my brother, not anymore. And if you must be put in jaws sharp enough to bleed the heart from you, I'll gladly hand you to the Wolf to do so.'"

Nesi felt his hand begin to shake in hers, as though the bones themselves wished to escape all confines of flesh and blood.

"I had heard we carried something special onboard, but I didn't know what until she had it brought out. It was supposed to be some sort of . . . I don't know. Torture device? A prize of some sort? The ship steward was livid, but my sister paid him no mind. She had a mission. Her soldiers stuffed me inside, but it was her that closed the helm over my head, smiling. From within, I could hear her enchanting it, growing spikes within to hold me fast, bands of metal to keep me silent. She was a powerful Speaker, had even earned her ink-rites back home in Kehora. With the Dawntongue glowing on her skin and hate in her blood, she commanded the armor to live, to live as I could not and would not. She wished so hard the sky boiled and the wood of the deck cracked beneath her. And then she was done.

"To this day, the way she looked at me as I was swallowed whole . . . Adera truly thought she was helping me."

He wiped his eyes, and could only stare at the armor that was his prison. "When we landed ashore two years ago, she went south, and I was taken north. Here. I'm kept under guard, but no one really cares anymore. It doesn't matter if I try to escape. It just . . . finds me every sunrise, no matter where I am. And it swallows me all over."

All at once he fell forward, exhausted by the telling, and she caught him. Nesi held Teor to her, as tight as she could, and felt her heart cracking in two as his story flooded through her, threatening to drown her.

The night whispered. From the moonlight and mist, T'sidaan appeared, crouched on the windowsill, watching them both with eyes like heated brass. Nesi looked at them, tears spilling down her face and then back at Teor. T'sidaan made a smooth, deep sound in the back of their throat, as they watched the young boy sob his story into Nesi's shoulder.

"Tyrants don't draw lines around clan or class; there is no one and no thing they will not take and use for their own ends. Especially their own. Especially those they feel should be grateful for the chance to be led blindly." T'sidaan took in a sharp breath, shook their head once, looked away. "My sibling never has to work very hard to convince mortals to conquer or hurt in his name. Often, the Wolf doesn't have to work at all. And when he does, the result is . . . brutal."

The way they spoke. Nesi watched as the light in their eyes became heavy with history, their mind going to some other time, some other place. The tales between Fox and Wolf were many but at a certain point in time, they simply . . . stopped. The story between them had ceased, untold. Nesi could almost see the intense weight of that untold story inside T'sidaan even now, coiled around their heart like ivy choking stone. Whatever had passed between them, Nesi understood all at once, would never be forgiven nor forgotten.

Nesi remembered that the Fox was the only Pillar actively fighting the Occupation. Seeing T'sidaan overwhelmed with this deep grief and rage for the first time in her audition, Nesi could only wonder at that untold story; somehow she knew, even if she asked, she'd never learn it.

Instead, she held Teor, who was so light in her arms, despite the heaviness of his past. "It all needs to come down, T'sidaan," she said, her voice cracking.

"It will," they responded, with the cryptic confidence of a fox framed in moonlight. "The flames of revolution live in the hearts of every Oranoyan too scared to fight back, every Zemini too scared to speak up. But fire is easy to dampen and temper, crush and quell, douse entirely. Far harder to stoke. Even harder to ignite."

In the breaking of Nesi's heart, doubt, sudden and sharp. "But it *will* happen, yes? It has to. I . . . I know it will! I've been on the other side of it. I've seen it! You've told me it will happen!"

Enigmatic, their gaze. For all their familiarity and trust in each other after all these months, they still had an aloofness that mystified and frightened her. "And who says the future is a given? What makes you think because it is how it's always happened that it's going to be how it always happens? You take causality for granted, young one. The future happens because we make it happen, because we *choose* for our best tomorrow to come. *That* is what I meant all those months ago in your cell on the first night here. The future is not a given. You must seize it or someone else will write it for you."

Anger flared up, hot, and held hands with the blooming doubt within her. "So, you're telling me it could all be for nothing? I've come this far, for what? It all to fail now?"

"Yes. Quite possibly." Their lips turned up into a smile, that goading grin they loved to use against her shaky faith. "What will you do about it, then?"

Nesi held the tired, exhausted form of Teor, whose sobbing had sent him into the lands of sleep, at least for a little while. This poor child of an unloving warlord, whose own family caged him in expectation, terror, and pain. How many more like him were forced to participate in horror until they grew numb and broken? How many more willingly joined, that needed to see justice for the evil they'd done? How many more days must her own people suffer, their story taken from them and a different one writ across their souls?

The plan came together in her mind like a shattered window in reverse, each piece fitting together just so in order to make a whole mosaic. Her eyes locked on the armor she'd spent months hating, silent and unoccupied. Nesi looked back at T'sidaan, whose tail swished back and forth in anticipation.

She wiped her eyes and nodded; heart restored.

She didn't give up. If she was going to fail, it would be on her feet.

"I'm going to make sure tomorrow comes. But I'm going to need your help."

T'sidaan blinked once, then with a bow, they said,

"Ooh, fascinating. I haven't had a proper team-up in ages, not since that debacle with the Butterfly and the dragons. And that was with Gren'hass and he's been around for some crises, let me tell you."

Their bright eyes of gold narrowed, like a predator before the pounce. "This is it, then? You feel ready?"

Nesi shrugged, attempted a half-grin, landed somewhere around a quarter. Her breath steamed in the cold before her. "No, I don't feel ready at all. But I don't think I ever will. Maybe it's what I've been missing the whole time, because . . . yeah, there has been exactly no point in all this that I've felt ready. Where answers arrived, and clarity struck, and you put a crown on my head or something and said, 'Congratulations, you did it!' I guess I just . . . have reached a point where someone has to do something, and if I'm not that someone, nothing will happen and nothing will get better, or have the hope of getting better. So, no, I'm sure as hells not ready. Which is why I know it's time to start moving anyway."

T'sidaan said nothing. They simply nodded once, and in their eyes, a light like pride shimmered in the gold of their gaze. "Let's move, then. Together."

Nesi found a full smile waiting, despite the despair, the wringing of her heart for Teor and her people, and all of this. She smiled at this god who had taken a chance on her and she knew: no matter what happened next, something was different now.

She and T'sidaan took the sleeping form of Teor into the living room and began to plan.

A TALE BETWEEN PILLARS

THE FOX AND THE STALLION

I<small>N THE DAYS BEFORE</small> you and I were brought forth from clay and cloud, the Fox of Tricks issued a challenge to the Stallion of Swiftness.

This did not happen often. The Fox prefers stealth and subterfuge, nipping at heels passing by the underbrush of the world. Direct challenges were not how they spent their days. The Fox, as we know, works better in the shadows cast by the sun, not the sun itself.

Except Danda'oon, the Stallion of Swiftness, had piqued their ire. A chestnut and gold stallion of remarkable size, Danda'oon was a god of the quick and the mighty, with candles lit by athletes, doctors, and soldiers, all those for whom an extra moment of alacrity could save a life. In those early days of the world, the Stallion had many candles lit in his name.

And in their glow, he grew proud and boastful.

Word had reached the Fox that their brother had grown arrogant, willfully pushing his worshippers past the point of exhaustion, commanding them to keep up with their god. Children grew sick. Adults fell, crumpling to earth or snow or stone like paper dolls. Even those able to keep up could only collapse after sunset and wake before its rise, marching on, their lives dedicated to the pace commanded of them.

Danda'oon had become a tyrant, and the Fox abhorred tyrants. You will remember this from the many tales of the Fox and the Wolf.

Into the camp of the Stallion, they appeared in robes of gold and cream and pumpkin and went to their brother, who pranced and whinnied at the heart of a dance by his dedicants. Emaciated as they were, the Fox felt sorrow seeing how high these clay and cloudlings leapt for their lord. Too much faith could wear away a mortal life, the Fox knew.

With a snap of their fingers, each torch flared bright, burning white as lilies. They did not shout, for that was not their way, but said , "Brother. I see you dance even as your people starve. Are you not ashamed?"

The drums ceased their discussion. The reed flutes went quiet. And the Stallion imperiously nosed aside his followers to stand before his sibling. The Fox's brother snorted with amusement. He'd forgotten how small his sibling was; half his mighty stature? Less than half! And just like them, to be the fly buzzing about his silken tail.

"Well, well, well, look who's emerged from their rotten log! My little sibling, come to make my worship their business. Are you prickly sister Hedgehog, sticking her little snout into every gutter for gossip? Or sibling

Hound, digging through the world's trash? Pray reveal your purpose, sibling, or leave."

If he meant to illicit anger, he failed. Foxes have thick fur and even thicker skin; besides, only the weak took offense at comparison. The Fox looked around the camp and saw many already unconscious from the dance and the day's toll.

Looking their brother in his wide, amber eye, they said, "Your followers are fearful of you and your displeasure. They are not able to keep up with your stride, and still, you push them to the brink of death. You need to stop, brother."

Danda'oon laughed and his bray could've come from the king of asses himself. "Please! Mortals are many. They couple and multiply and come the spring, I will have more. Why need I worry about those who cannot keep up with my lightning stride? If they do not wish to join the race, they may stay behind."

The Fox shook their head, gesturing to the many deerskin tents and cookfires. "You have families following you, brother. They cannot stay behind, not when they rely on you to give them protection. Have you no heart? No compassion? No one has ever danced for me and if they did, I doubt it would be with half the passion your dedicants have for you. Why do you treat them ill?"

Danda'oon stamped the ground hard, the earth tremble with his offense. "That's right," he said, voice heavy as his shoes, "no one *has* ever danced for you. Why *would* they? You bring mischief and leave chaos in your wake. Who in their right mind would light a candle for you, little kit? Even one of my dedicants is worth more to me than you are; they at least keep sight of my flank and you, why you would not move fast enough to event taste the dust of my passing."

And though he didn't know it, Danda'oon had made a mistake. He'd open the door for T'sidaan to look him in the eye and say, "Why, that sounds like quite the challenge, brother. And I've always enjoyed a good challenge." Their eyes flashed molten gold as they raised their voice. "A challenge, then! I will race you from sea to sea. If I beat you, you will show your worshippers the respect they are owed. If you beat me, I will dance for you every night for a year and a day."

The Stallion of Swiftness wasted no time in snorting, "I accept this challenge! And I look forward to seeing you leap and bound in my name. Name your time and place."

The Fox grinned, a sickle of moonlight seeming to gleam in their fangs. "In a day's time, I will meet you at the northernmost tip of the Snowtemper Sea at sunrise. We will race the length and breadth of this land. Whosoever's toe touches the sands of the Iyan Coast first will be winner. I ask you give your worshippers a day of rest while we compete. Let them lounge along the route we'll tread. This is between Pillars."

Danda'oon tossed his head and laughed. From coast to coast? Why there were sea winds that traveled that distance slower than he! Again, his sibling proved themself a fool.

"Deal! Back to your hole, sibling. Enjoy its warmth for a final night, for the day after tomorrow, you will be too busy dancing for me to do much else."

In his arrogance and dismissal, the Stallion missed the Fox's grin morph into a full and menacing smile.

T'sidaan, of course, did not go back to the Woods of the World.

They walked into the dark and changed shape, easy as the wind changed direction or leaves changed their color. They knew what their brother did not and would never understand: all creatures that thrived on pride held in their hearts a deep and terrible fear.

But any armor built to hide that fear would always be brittle, pried open as much by words as by blades.

And the Fox was a master of words.

They clad themself as a woman, buxom and blushing, hourglassed and athletic, walking among the tired masses of the Stallion's dedicants. Over bowls of thin soup and weak ale, they said in a voice like a ringing bell, "Oh, but that tricksy Fox! Faster than you'd think and twice as clever. But not so clever they don't have a weakness. I hear that they cannot stand the scent or taste or even the mere presence of peaches, for a fruit of the spring, that season which is their opposite, will cause the Fox to slow and shy away!"

And the people of the Stallion listened and told their lord.

Walking out of another shadow, they clad themself as a man, tall as a tree and wide as a stone, with muscles like corded wood and a face chiseled and strong. At laundry lines and over cookpits, they said in a voice like a hammer strike, "Oh, but that Fox, stronger than they look and twice as smart. But not so strong that they don't have a weakness. I hear that the very sight of dogs will make them fall back on instinct, fearful and weeping at being chased. Why even the smell of dog shit is enough to make them wobbly in the knees and slow!"

And the people of the Stallion listened and told their lord.

On and on it went all night, the Fox appearing in forms of men, women, and various people of all kinds, whispering in the ears of the dedicants, knowing that they would report back to their lord, fearing his wrath more than the Fox's own gambit for their freedom.

Well, the Fox never did what they did to be thanked or danced for, and so took no offense.

In a day's time, they waited patiently on the beach of the Snowtemper Sea, standing astride the massive obsidian rock that would welcome the Swan Armada in a century's time. When Danda'oon and some of his worshippers appeared over the horizon, T'sidaan did not smile, for they were a very good actor, but looked on in delight as their brother trotted toward them.

His chestnut coat was filthy, smeared with a truly extraordinary amount of feces, the air itself wilting from the foul scent. His mane was soaked in urine, a dripping, light yellow and now a stain on the massive horse.

And with a "Good morning to you, dearest sibling!" the Fox felt more than smelled a noxious wave of fresh peaches digesting within the belly of their brother. Bits of macerated flesh and skin were still in his teeth. His muzzle, too, was smeared with peach juice and around his neck a garland of the fruit sat heavy, making his head hang low.

"Are you surprised I've learned of your weaknesses? For am I not a Stallion of Swiftness and does not my mind race with knowledge? If you wish to call off this little challenge between us, for you shall be too fearful to even move a foot in my presence, I understand! Why, I won't even make you start dancing for a full day's time!"

The Fox remained stoic. "Oh, brother mine, however did you learn of my weaknesses? Why, I thought I had buried the secret of peaches and dogs."

Even covered in shit and reeking of peaches, the Stallion didn't bother crediting his dedicants for their help. "Well, you thought wrong, sibling. And here, wreathed in your fear, will I win our challenge!"

If the Stallion noticed his present horde of followers standing away from him than usual, he did not say. Nor did he remark on how every so often, one of them would clap a hand to their mouth, stifling a laugh at their prancing lord covered in shit, whose farts reeked like a wet, spring orchard.

The Fox hopped off the massive rock and brushed themself off, nodding at their brother. "Well, then, my doom is surely at hand. Shall we get this over with?"

Danda'oon reared up on his hind legs, his mighty shit-stained forelegs swiping at the air. "I'll see you on the southern coast, sibling!"

Then, with all the canniness of a child attempting to trick an adult, Danda'oon began to walk behind T'sidaan, the Fox taking their time walking up the beach and toward land. Eventually, the Fox looked back, a mild expression of concern on their face. "Oh, brother,

I think you're doing it wrong. Are you not supposed to speed ahead of me?"

The Stallion's smile was fevered with victory. "You wish I would do such a thing! But the moment I'm gone, you will simply slip into the Woods of the World and beat me there. No, I will hound you the whole way until you must flee, cudgeled by my weapons!"

A little shrug of their orange and cream shoulder. "I may as well give up now from the sound of it, terrified as I am. And yet, I'm a Pillar of my word. I will see through your challenge." And they walked on.

For the first hundred miles, Danda'oon's scattered dedicants watched their god move as slow as a snail, creeping just behind the Fox, covered in dog shit, urine, his belly full of fruit; too much fruit. With little heed to how ridiculous he looked and how terribly he reeked, Danda'oon crawled on, growing more and more furious over the lack of fear in his sibling.

He began to grind and swallow the garland of peaches around his neck, shouting in desperation, "Shit! More shit! I am losing my foulness!"

But both were bad ideas. For the new peaches in his stomach sent the old ones tumbling out of his ass in great heaps, rancid and loose, his hooves catching in it, causing the Stallion of Swiftness to slip and fall into his own excrement.

By two hundred miles, dogs of all kinds had begun to appear, following the sweet aroma of peach shit curious. "Ah-ha!" cried Danda'oon, who had yet to stop shitting, "Look, more hounds! I can sense your terror from here, sibling. You had best run!"

T'sidaan watched dozens of dogs rubbing themselves on their brother's body, sniffing and licking and wagging their many tails in excitement. "They seem more interested in you than me, brother. But I will be careful when they realize who it is you're pursuing."

And when they laughed, all of Danda'oon's dedicants laughed with them. It was now the Stallion saw how all his followers had joined the Fox; no one stood by his side.

By three hundred miles, Danda'oon had emptied his stomach and rain had washed much of the shit from his body. His followers stayed with the Fox, and no dogs hounded him, instead running after the Fox. And somewhere in all of his distress, the Fox had raced ahead with Danda'oon's followers, laughing and leaping.

Danda'oon felt empty.

And maybe for the first time ever, he was scared. He had never been alone before.

As his hooves finally met the sands of the Iyan Coast, he sat down, engulfed by sorrow. For a part of him knew: this was how he made his followers feel all the time. Shame rushed in like the tide and Danda'oon, Stallion of Swiftness, wept.

As the sun set, a voice spoke above Danda'oon. "Brother."

He could not meet the Fox's gaze. "Yes, sibling?"

"You've learned your lesson."

"I have," he responded, though they had not asked a question.

"We are gods, brother. Responsible to those who love us. If you will not take care of those who light their candles for you, I will be here to remind you what that loneliness feels like, to feel neglect when someone more powerful than you could fix it with a moment's attention. Is that understood?"

He nodded, silent.

T'sidaan squatted and looked their brother in the eye. "Treat your worshippers with care, and they will do the same for you. And remember, brother: tyrants earn poor treatment, but the earnest are loved, flaws and all."

The Fox stood and left, wandering away from their brother. They did not stay to see Danda'oon's followers approach with fresh water and a soft blanket for their Pillar. But they did hear him cry out with shame, with relief, apologizing over and over again to those that loved him.

Danda'oon never again mistreated his followers and took care of them everywhere they went. If ever anyone fell behind, he would let them ride his back, and he would ask their name and where they were from.

If anyone ever asked him of that day with the Fox, the Stallion would not balk from the truth. "I was acting foolish and my sibling proved me a fool. Let it not be said that even gods cannot grow or change."

And somewhere deep within the Woods of the World, the Fox would hear this and they would smile, right before enjoying a bite of a succulent, ripe springtime peach.

—From Aecrades' *Clay and Cloud Tales: Volume III*

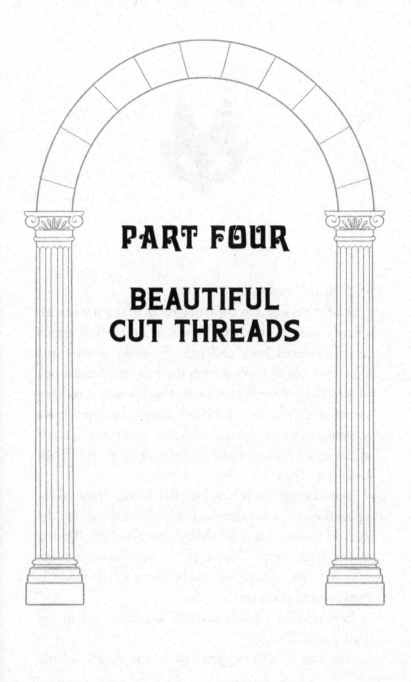

PART FOUR

BEAUTIFUL CUT THREADS

"Don't panic."

Nesi stood in the living room of the tower with a newly awoken Teor, who leaned on a makeshift crutch for his twisted back and legs. Standing nearby was Una, eyes warily moving from the pale, red-headed boy to Nesi to the looming armor, and back again. "You keep saying don't panic. But what if that's the appropriate response to being brought into this tower at the crack of dawn, la? Den of some drakeshade monster?" Then looking at Teor, "No offense, of course."

Teor shrugged and raised his free hand. "None taken, I promise you. I feel the same way about the thing," he said. His voice was solid though his eyes kept flicking to the armor with a sense of tension. "Though Nesi, whatever you want to say, maybe hurry a little before it awakens and takes me?"

Nesi nodded. Now or never. "Okay. Just . . . okay, just don't panic. T'sidaan?"

The Fox of Tricks appeared in the middle of the

room in a burst of magic. Nesi had asked to keep the dramatics to a minimum and so when they emerged in a puff of purple and gold smoke, a fan of peacock feathers in one hand, the other flourished above them, posing like a dancer on their back leg while starbursts of light sparked about their head as they shouted, "Ta-da!" she realized the two of them had vastly different ideas of minimum.

Una gasped, dropping to her knees, head bowing so fast she almost slammed into the floor.

Teor jumped back, catching himself on a wall, eyes wide and filled with a curious fear that he hadn't even shown for his iron prison.

Nesi palmed her forehead and sighed. "This is your idea of minimum?"

T'sidaan pouted, dismissing the smoke, fan, and starbursts. "What? Not enough sparkles or too many?" Then they looked down and saw Una. "Uh oh, one moment."

Crouching, they put a delicate black nail under Una's chin, interrupting a soft babble of what sounded like prayer. "Darling," they said, whispering, "it makes me ever so happy to see such reverence for a Pillar of Heaven, but I might in fact be the very last of my family who'd smile to see such swift obeisance, especially to such a fool as I. And your smile is far too bright to be obscured by floorboards. Please arise."

When she didn't move and kept praying, the Fox shook their head, tsking. Looking at Teor, they said with a wink, "Why I'm positively drowning in dedicants, what a burden." Nesi watched as Teor clamped his mouth shut, lips paling with the effort, unsure whether to laugh or scream. T'sidaan's smile didn't wane but their eyes softened.

To Una, they sighed and said, "With gratitude, I release you. In freedom, I bid you stand, and know you stand strong as a Pillar, lei'me."

At the honorific of "child," Una looked up, eyes bright as though she may cry at any moment. "My Pillar. The honor is mine."

"Oh, it most certainly is, I promise you." They kissed her brow and said, "Up, up, up please, you're making me feel like a being with responsibilities and that is *not* my domain."

She stood, and looked at Nesi with awe. "You . . . you weren't lying. Or crazy!"

Nesi smiled. "Maybe a little crazy, but no. Not lying. I'm—" Here she looked at T'sidaan. She and the Fox had not discussed a cover story. How did you tell someone, "Hey did you know your life is an entrance exam for me three hundred years from now?"

Luckily, the Fox had a silver tongue when they weren't using it to be crude. "Nesi is a young acolyte from a small temple of dedicants cloistered away from the paved roads of central Oranoya. Originally an acolyte of the Bison, I seduced her away with my wily promise of fame and renown, but so far all she's done is learn how to inspire people and feel bad about things. Terrible, I know. But she's been a good and faithful student, and with her help inside this death trap of a fortress, I come now to aid her in her chosen mission: chasing away the Wolfhounds and their bastard kind. No offense," they said, smiling at Teor.

"None . . . none taken," he said, breathing hard. He was studying the Fox as though desperately trying to understand if he was seeing one of the Hundred Hammers of Hell, or if he was really seeing a god. "You're . . . you're real."

"Unfortunately," they said with a little shrug. "Don't feel odd if you're unhappy with such confirmation. Many of my siblings wish I were not real, too."

"No, no," he said, getting back to his feet and approaching on his crutch. A flicker of a grin crossed his pale face, the fear in his eyes turning to awe. "I'm . . . not unhappy. I'm just . . . I grew up on stories of you. Terrible, horrible tales. Stories of violence and malice, sharp teeth and cruel thoughts, and you're . . . none of those things. In fact, you seem like quite a dilettante, no offense."

Now it was T'sidaan's turn to laugh. "None taken! I can see how you'd get that impression with my subtle entrance and serious attitude. But I promise you, Teor of Zemin, when it comes to tricks, I am very serious indeed. And your country has been playing one on you your whole life."

Any other Zemini would have been insulted, but Nesi saw an understanding come over Teor's face, solemn and yet creased with an emotion Nesi could only describe as when someone truly feels seen for the first time. He nodded. "You're correct, Fox. And I suppose I've been a punchline so long it stopped being funny and just became . . . my life."

T'sidaan put a delicate hand on Teor's thin shoulder. "I know the feeling. It is a humbling thing to be the joke from time to time. But when those above you punch down, crushing you, smaller and smaller, enough to make you think your life is the joke? No greater cruelty in the world exists, as far as this jester is concerned. And for my part, on behalf of all Ninety-Nine Pillars of Heaven, I am very sorry my hateful brother made your home his den. And we will stop his war. Starting here. With that."

All four of them looked to the armor of Ogre.

T'sidaan flourished a hand at it. "Nesi?"

Nesi bowed, trying to feign some kind of reverence like Una had. "Of course. I think that this monstrosity is more than a weapon. It's become a symbol. I know all the Wolfhounds are brutal, but whatever your sister did to it, Teor, it doles out violence like rain clouds do the rain. The Oranoya see it as a thing to be feared, the Zeminis see it as a sign of their authority. And if we can take it apart, in front of as many people as possible, I think it's going to do exactly what I've been hoping this whole time."

"Which is?" Una asked.

"Remind everyone here that a harmful tool can be dismantled. And that we're no one's punchline or punching bag." Looking to Teor, she said, "But in order to do that, we'll need to take control of it, break whatever magic is within it. I don't suppose you've got any ideas on how to do that?"

Teor looked hopeful, but suddenly lost. "I think that all sounds like a good idea, Nesi. But . . . no. No, I've no mind for magic; the Dawntongue does not work in my voice. Believe me, I was always curious but my sister forbade it, as did my parents. And there is . . . something that was not there when she first encased me, but has only grown stronger."

Nesi looked to Una. Una shook her head from side to side. "I know exactly one magic trick, and the card usually falls out of my sleeve. I'm not your girl for this, Nesi."

It was then the Fox ambled toward the armor that dwarfed even their tall stature. They drank in its jagged points, its sharp edges, its hollow, dark interior.

A slow, delicate motion of their hand in front of the helm, and moving down its height. As they did so, Nesi gasped. Hundreds upon hundreds of luminous threads began to appear within the armor. Each glowed a faint indigo and silver light, like the underside of the full moon; the web of threads not only sat within the armor but, Nesi saw in horror as dozens of them flowed out, to Teor. As fine as silk, they bound him: wrists, ankles, throat, his middle, his fingers, even his eyelids, as though he would forever be a witness within the armor.

For the first time in their company, Nesi heard a deep, angry growl in the back of the Fox's throat. "Well," they said, their normally light voice gone dark and hot, "it seems my sister did choose a side." Turning back to the four of them, they said, "I'd recognize the Spider's weave anywhere; she always works with a spiteful little flair. When your sister started her ritual, I have no doubt Nera'Je saw it as an opportunity to gift divine aid without declaring for our excommunicated brother."

With a sigh, T'sidaan turned back, the threads fading. "I cannot cut these. Her workings have lingered within for too long, and if she feels my nails attempting to snap even one, I have no doubt she'll retaliate with . . . unnecessary force." Teor didn't see it, but Nesi caught the Fox quickly glance at the thread around his throat and then look away.

"So that's it?" she asked. "Back to the drawing board?"

The Fox stroked their chin. Then, "No, not necessarily. I will just have to call in a favor."

"I would call that favor quickly, my Pillar," Una said. "I don't think the Ogre is going to wait for us before it tries to eat its breakfast."

A finger on the gauntlet twitched as the growing dawn light touched it.

"Ah," the Fox said. From their sleeve, they pulled a handful of sand. With a wave of their arm, hot, golden sand scattered over the armor, making the threads visible once more.

The armor froze and Teor sighed with relief. "What was that?" he asked.

"Oh, just a little slumber dust from my brother Agi'uhn, the Koala of Sleep. The sand under his tree is good for a snooze, and I'll replace it before he wakes sometime next century. It won't hold forever against my Nera'Je's workings, but it should be enough while we ask for a little help."

Turning to Nesi, they said, "Now, a test, my young acolyte. My sister's workings, which sibling of mine should you call? Who in the family with no allegiance to my sister, my hateful brother, and who'd not immediately spit in your face when they see me?"

Nesi went through the long list of gods she knew,

weighed domains against temperaments. She studied Teor's fear, deep furrows of age carving themselves into his young face from years of torment. She pondered Una's beautiful hands, raw, cracked, and bleeding from the horror that had become her norm. She thought of the Spider and the Wolf, how dedication and the hunt could merge to create purposeful violence, two domains that lent their worst to each other, alchemizing into something even worse.

She thought of the only thing that could cut through these threads that bound them all.

Bringing her hands into prayer-form, Nesi touched that divine well within her that connected her to the Pillars of Heaven.

"Eleth'rao, Hawk of Justice, I call you by my heart's candle. In the name of T'sidaan the Fox of Tricks, I beseech your aid in correcting a grave injustice."

A moment passed.

Then, a high-pitched screech arose from the window.

T'sidaan smiled at Nesi. "A very wise choice, my acolyte," Then, leaning in, they whispered, "I'm not going to piss her off for a while, so excellent timing, quite literally." To the Hawk, they said, "Sister! Your presence is welcome."

She was absolutely enormous, and truly beautiful. Talons of gold gripped splintered wood. Eyes of pure shadow scanned the room. Her beak was a burnished bronze point.

But it was her feathers that took the breath away. A cascading waterfall of gray and brown and gold that started from a crest of marigold at her head, a cycle of color Nesi knew would match sky, earth, and sea, wherever she flew, she'd remain present but hidden, until the time to strike came.

When Nesi blinked, the Hawk was gone.

As tall as T'sidaan, her black skin wreathed with garlands of feathers, her brow bald and smooth, Eleth'rao stunned in her human guise. These eyes shone like motes of fire, these nails ending in wicked, sharp hooks. A strong nose profiled her, regal and keen, and her shoulders were so well-defined, Nesi felt Una start sweating from the overwhelming beauty of the goddess of Justice.

T'sidaan looked back and chuckled. Then to their sister, "Oh Eleth'rao, your plumage never does cease to enthrall the clay and cloudlings." Then, they bowed. "Your aid is appreciated, sister. Though it was understood our family would pick no sides, it seems some siblings like the taste of falsehoods first, and truth second."

The Hawk stood silent for a full minute, drinking in every detail before looking at her sibling with weary whimsy. "That you'd complain of Nera'Je picking a side when you're so actively, and boldly, meddling is . . . not surprising, but surely even you can taste the irony of the moment, dear sibling."

"Oh, sister, by our siblings, shame on you! I was born to meddle, I carved myself away from the stone for the express purpose of meddling. I deserve a medal for all the meddling I do. If I'm not meddling, the universe collapses! I see why you find it funny, but I take umbrage with our sister meddling when that is expressly my domain. Besides," they added, their voice moving back to that place of raw anger, "you know as well as anyone, I have good reason to meddle. The best of them."

Nesi watched the Hawk soften, if a being so powerful and sharp could be said to have softness in them. Before she could say anything, T'sidaan continued, "And all that aside, you cannot look at her work here and call it anything but injustice, can you?"

Again, those eyes of fire. Teor staggered back, as though even her attention was sharp enough to pin him to the wall. After drinking in the threads that bound him, she shook her head from side to side. "No. It is not justice."

To Teor, she said, "And when you are free, will you work to free others in turn?"

For the first time, Nesi saw him stand as straight as he could, and though he was not war-like, she knew he had courage in him. He summoned it now to say, "Yes. It has always been my desire. Freedom earned is freedom given. I would do my best to keep doing that work."

She nodded, satisfied, though her face remained passive. "Good. Then the cycle of justice continues." From her garland of feathers, she turned to Nesi and plucked a single pinion. It was steel gray, and Nesi's vision swam, as it became a knife, then a feather, and then a knife being handed over, hilt first. "Use my feather to free this boy. When you are done, burn it. It shall return to me."

Then, moving to T'sidaan, she embraced them, and kissed them on the cheek. "I take my leave, sibling. I hope to feast with you again someday at our Heavenly Table. I miss your stories so."

T'sidaan looked uncomfortable, even as they returned the embrace. Nesi felt for them. She wasn't used to people expressing care to her either, especially with an audience. "Yes, yes," they said, "I'll do my best, but you know me. Quite busy. Always busy. Never a moment's rest for the wicked such as I. Already, a fiddle contest scheduled with brother Cricket tomorrow, wouldn't you know? Family dinners usually wind up toward the bottom of my extensive list but . . . but I will try. Though I fear you'll tire of me long before you tire of my stories."

Eleth'rao smiled the smile of a sister who knew when their sibling was joking to hide a feeling. Nesi recognized it as one Authoritative Ren used exclusively for her, and suddenly felt very seen, which she hated.

The Hawk stepped back and bowed to Nesi. "A pleasure to see you again, Nesi. I am glad to see you've found the right wind beneath your wings."

Oh, right. Pillars existed across time. Damn, she remembered Nesi and doubtless she remembered Nesi's poor audition. She bowed, even as her cheeks burned. "Just needed to find the right blowhard, my Pillar."

The Hawk's laugh was as shrill as her predator's cry. She smiled as she went to the window. "Okay. That was a good one." Then in a hawk's cry and a rush of air, she was gone.

The Fox looked back at Teor sullenly, ears twitching in annoyance. "See? Being the joke once in a while can be humbling. Sometimes," they said, pointedly at Nesi. "Now, let us begin the delicate work."

Nesi held the Hawk's knife before her, staring at it

with a grimace. She was not someone who held knives often, not even for kitchen duty. The traits of clumsy and anxious did not often go well with adjectives like sharp and heavy. She looked at Teor. "Uh, how good are you at holding still?"

She didn't think the poor boy could look paler and yet he did, losing almost all color from his face. Una put her head in her hands. "Toad's cursed eye! You're going to kill the poor boy, look at him, he's shaking!"

T'sidaan raised their hands and made shushing sounds at Teor, like you might to a frightened pony. "Here's what we're going to do. You, Teor," they said, grabbing a humble stool from the nearby table, "are going to sit. You, Una, are going to stand guard and watch for anyone coming this way. And you, Nesi," they said, "are going to go very slowly, very carefully, and not chop off Teor's head, hands, or genitals. Deal?"

All three of them nodded.

Una went outside, muttering a prayer to the Dove of Health.

Teor sat down, hands white-knuckled on the wooden stool.

Nesi approached with the knife and tried to remember how to breathe.

The first was the hardest. Even with the sand, finding the nearly invisible threads of the Spider took effort. But when she did, she moved at a pace to make the Snail proud. When the knife of justice pressed against the thread, it felt solid, as though it were made of steel and not silk.

But then the knife blurred and cut through the thread,

which snapped apart with a twang like an out of tune mandolin.

As as it broke, Teor took a deep breath in, his face full of awe. Nesi knew that thread around his neck had probably been choking him for so long, that he had forgotten what it was like to breathe as a free person.

Still, he didn't tremble less. In fact, the more Nesi cut, the worse he became.

She couldn't stop to calm him, so she looked to T'sidaan. With a gentle smile, the Fox took a few steps into the air, and sat cross-legged beside Teor. "Teor," they said, "distract me. Watching Nesi work is boring as rocks. Do you have a favorite story or poem you could trade me?"

Teor's eyes flicked to them, and a faint smile appeared, then left. "Oh, I—I have a poem I wrote. Would that do? I'm fond of it, though I can tell it's middling at best."

From any other Pillar that widening of eyes, *sudden delight*, might be read as derision or sarcasm. But when T'sidaan leaned forward and said, "Your own poetry? *And* it's middling? Oh, please share! It would be a delight," Nesi believed them.

Teor laughed, and for the first time, Nesi saw a little joy appear from the hope of sharing his passion, and she hated his family that much more, that they'd made their boy think that joy was somehow wrong.

Twang went another thread as Teor continued. "I . . . I call this one 'By Thresher's Hands Alone.'" He went still, eyes closed, plumbing the depths of his memory. Then:

"Favored blade of nature's reaping
Turned upon earth's labors, sleeping
From dreams torn, chaff and wheat
The womb of soil, fall and meet
Helpless bounty sits at farmer's feet
Their tears of sorrow he happy greets
The belly of killers, into that safe keeping
Shall the children of earth meet their reaping"

Teor stopped, opened his eyes, and looked at the Fox. It seemed he'd recited enough poetry to not let hope enter his eyes, and Nesi's heart went out to him.

All too quickly, he learned what Nesi had learned: T'sidaan was a good liar, but they were not delicate when it came to the truth.

"Hmm," they said, nodding in appreciation. "You're right, that *was* middling!"

"Oh," Teor said. *Twang* went another thread. "Really?"

"Oh yes, quite. Right down the middle, oh stalwart poet. I loved it!"

"You—wait, what?" Teor scrunched up his eyebrows in confusion. "But you agreed it was middling."

T'sidaan nodded, happy and seeming to enjoy Teor's confusion. "Not just middling; quite middling! But since I have no reason to lie to you, middling art tends to be my favorite kind. Poetry, fiction, movies—I mean plays, all of it I prefer middling, though, I of course enjoy great art and love tearing bad art to pieces."

Through the door, Una's voice, muffled. "Why? Yes, I've been listening, so what?"

The Fox barked a laugh as Nesi shook her head. She

could tell a ramble was coming, and they did not disappoint. "Because middling art is the most inspiring kind of art! When something is awful, it's a joke; a bad piece of art makes people talk, sure, but it's always in scorn or derision. No one experiences truly ghastly art and wants to improve it. And the same with truly beautiful work. Those heights of achievement are exquisite and capture something ecstatic in the universe, yes. But if one measures themselves against greatness, they'll always be upset at themselves for not matching it, because few do. But!" they held up a pristine nail and winked at Teor, "middling art? Art that has strong qualities while still not quite capturing greatness? That is the best kind of art, my friend. And why I love your poetry and that you write it. Because a very bad poet will see your art and wish to try harder. A very good poet will see your art and try to be better. And someone who has never made any art at all will see your art and know it's possible for them to try, too. For my money, that last is the most valuable. We could all stand to create more than we destroy, especially these days. Even if it *is* middling. So take heart, Teor. You may be the most important person in this room, because no matter what you do, it's going to be inspiring."

Nesi kept at her methodical work, but out of the corner of her eye, she saw Teor blush and smile deeply, and she wondered just how long it had been since anyone had shown him kindness.

After a moment, he said, "I can only express my gratitude, Fox. I'm . . . overwhelmed. You're nothing like what I heard growing up. In Zemin, we're raised on stories meant to terrify. To make the world outside of Zemin upsetting, backward, just . . . wrong." Looking to Nesi, he said, "I thought all Oranoyan were cold, calculating, elitist monsters who would let a gosling drown if they had the final chapter of a book left to enjoy. And you," he said, looking at T'sidaan, "Well . . . worse than a monster. Monsters cannot help but be what they are, but the Fox, we were taught, always knew what they were doing. Always chose cruelty, always chose hurt. Knew no mercy, would never cede to another's pleas. We have many tales of the Spurning Divine, who we were told drove their brother away, but Zemin children know the Fox couldn't be trusted, or given quarter. But . . . clearly that's not true. What . . . I mean, if I could . . . why do they tell such awful den tales?"

Una gasped at the possible insolence, but Nesi studied her mentor. She didn't think they'd be upset; when you grew fearing a god and upon meeting them realized they were both kind and kind of a clown, she was sure it wouldn't be odd to want to know more.

A pained look crossed T'sidaan's face. Nesi recognized it. She'd seen it several times before, a crease in their brow, a subtle lifting of the black lip to show their canine. Often, they would simply fade away, and return a day or two later, as though nothing had happened.

But here, T'sidaan remained. When they finally spoke, their voice held a heavy weariness.

"There are some stories seldom told, younglings, for mortals and for Pillars. Not because they are too lurid or too dangerous, but because they . . . hurt. They hurt too much."

Nesi paused and locked eyes with the Fox. They held her gaze, and she saw no trick, no mirth, maybe even some fear. It could be a terrifying thing, sincerity, especially if you were so used to hiding from it.

In the Fox's eyes, Nesi saw pain, and beyond that, she saw a question.

Nesi nodded, giving her answer. Teor and Una did the same.

Even gods need permission to share their wounds, she thought.

In a very soft voice, T'sidaan said, "This is the last time I saw him, my brother. The last and the worst. My brutal brother, who broke me in half, and half again. I will tell you the final tale of the Fox and the Wolf."

And then, they told a story.

When they finished, the room was silent as a grave, the only sound a final *twang* of thread snapping as Nesi finished.

With no noise whatsoever, as though in respect to T'sidaan's tale, the armor disassembled in silence. Bereft of enchantment, it collapsed gently into a neat pile, the painted wolf on the helm facing away.

The knife in Nesi's hand was sharp enough to quiet any heart it was aimed at; she'd always pondered on the strength needed to kill.

But in the aftermath of the tale, she knew: the greater strength was choosing not to kill at all.

Facing the Fox, Nesi placed the knife on the floor, watching as they wiped away tears. Said, "I'm ... so sorry, T'sidaan." The tension in their body was great, as though they may vanish at any moment.

They released a long, low breath. When they opened their eyes, they nodded. "Thank you, Nesi. Given all you and I have been through, the difficulties asked of our friends here, it didn't feel right leaving this particular story . . . neglected."

There must have been a look on her face because they pointed a nail at her. "Hug me at your peril, mortal. I mean it. An embrace from my sister is a bad enough way to begin my day, don't you dare attempt anything heartfelt either."

Nesi smiled. "Well, I wouldn't dare attempt to annoy the legendary annoyance."

T'sidaan sniffed in mock disdain. "Exactly. There you have it."

Teor had gotten up as they spoke, not knowing what to do, but compelled to inspect the armor that had been his cage for the last year. "Wow," he breathed. "It's done."

"Nah, kuyo," Una said, coming up next to him and supporting his elbow, "something tells me it's only just beginning.

Nesi joined them, standing over the broken shell of this monster, a symbol of the ones who had hurt each and every one of them standing in the tower room. She nodded, then looked back at T'sidaan.

The Fox put their hands in their robe sleeves. A light of determination had replaced the pain in their trickster's eye. "That it is, dear Una. Nesi? The future is in your hands."

"Not just mine," she said, reaching for Teor and Una's, "ours."

The three of them held hands, and T'sidaan smiled to see it. "Very well. Lead on then, my acolyte."

A gust of winter wind came through the window, and the chill that ran down her spine reminded Nesi of the stakes. Time was running out. The revolution had to come and soon.

But she had allies. A mentor. Tools to be used.

And most importantly, a secret she'd been holding all this time that, if used correctly, would do exactly that.

"First things first," she said. "We're going to need fabric. Whole bolts if we can get it. Una, I'll need a rotation of kitchen staff and pages you trust. And finally? We're going to need tuskweed. A lot of it."

Each of them set into motion as the Fox stepped back into the shadows and watched their acolyte work toward the end of their audition.

A TALE BETWEEN PILLARS

THE FOX AND THE WOLF

I<small>N THE DAYS</small> before the Wolf of the Hunt was banished from the pantheon, the Fox of Tricks made a vow to kill him. There are many tales between the Fox and the Wolf, stories of deception and trickery, violence and pain, sorrow and rage.

This is the last one. At least, last for now.

And I heard it directly from the mouth of the mournful Fox themself.

They had closed their eyes before beginning; that alone chilled me. It was the first time I'd ever seen them do that—becoming still in their storytelling rather than spinning up in their usual animation.

T'sidaan told us they hold this story deep within their heart, a flame forever burning on hatred alone. They admitted, almost with shame, this story is the reason they stopped taking acolytes for such a long while, preferring solitude for many, many years. They said that any inquiry, even from one of their divine siblings, invites their endless ire, for no recounting of this tale brings them peace. To even be reminded it happened brings them pain, every time. That they told us at all spoke to the importance of this moment, their vulnerability, their deep emotion.

It is a story they may very well never tell again, and so I whisper it to you now, whoever you are, for they must not know you know. Even still, it is a brief tale, and sad.

All I can say as preface is that in the telling two things happened: my heart broke, utterly. And where the pieces fell, they landed in those empty spaces of the Fox's story, filling them in. Bringing understanding. Terrible understanding.

One day, the Wolf, whose name has been torn from the minds of man, decided he was tired of being tricked. He was tired of being one step behind his fleet-footed sibling, who tweaked his nose and stuck thorns in his paws and taunted him mercilessly before his dedicants. The Wolf was tired of being a joke. It didn't matter that that was how the Fox treated all his ninety-eight siblings, that many humored their sibling, for wasn't this the nature of T'sidaan? Better to ask the sun to set in the east, easier to convince oceans to fly and stone to flow than ask the Fox to change.

It didn't matter to him. He would finally make the Fox listen.

The Wolf was adamant in his pain.

And a wolf in pain will snap at whatever is nearest.

No matter how small. No matter how helpless. Or innocent.

T'sidaan paused, and I've never seen them at a loss for words until now. When they continued, their voice was low, their gaze lost to memory, and to even get through the telling, the Fox retreated from the first-person and found safety in third-person's distance.

The Fox was gone only a moment. But a jaw needs even less time than that to close, to grind, to swallow.

When the Fox returned, their child was gone.

A kit so young, they hadn't even dreamed of a name yet.

Una had gasped, hands to her lips. Teor's mouth dropped open, his eyes watering at the thought of such horrendous loss. I was still. If I could do anything, let me honor them, T'sidaan and nameless young both, with silent, reverent stillness.

Who they would have become, what those scant few weeks of whirlwind existence together hinted at as parent and child loped through the eternal autumn of home . . . all gone in the closing of a hateful jaw.

It's funny, I suppose, that the Wolf had had a whole monologue planned out. A recounting of ill deeds and humiliations and more and more, a vicious belittling culminating in the reasoning as to why he would dare devour their young, dare to commit familicide.

See the lesson? he'd say, not triumphant but matter of fact. *See how actions have consequences? You, who elude them like fish dashing from the net, cannot escape this one. And if you will not pay for them, others shall incur the price of your trickery and insult. This, the lesson, sibling. Learn it well, for if you do not, I will teach you in the shape of violence every time.*

And he planned to grin, to lick their child's life from his dripping jaw, and laugh.

That is what he would have said. In all their life, the Fox had never been one for violence.

But the Wolf was not prepared for the ferocity of a grieving parent.

To recount their fight would take more time than we have, my friend. To even call it a fight is . . . ill-fitting; fights are fair. This rush of violence, this flood of grief shaped by tooth and claw, was no such thing. Even that which T'sidaan hinted at is enough to bring a shiver to my spine, still.

For a year and a day, the Wolf of the Hunt knew what it was to become hunted. In a wordless hiss of rage, T'sidaan vowed to kill their sibling. Across the map of Oranoya and beyond, he knew no peace and found no safe harbor from the fury of the Fox, no sibling daring to give the Wolf refuge. T'sidaan, whose implacable will saw them outwit dragons and outsmart kings, had been bent toward the beating heart of their kin. It would not unbend until it was still and he was dead.

On the shores of what would become Zemin, they cornered the Wolf, bloody, beaten, and a heartbeat away from his end. No one would be surprised for the story to come to its foregone, even earned, conclusion.

Oh, the look in their eye. I still can't forget it. I don't wish to, even though it hurts. To be at the crossroad of memory and still wonder if the right path had been taken. That look was there now. And for the life of me, I couldn't tell if T'sidaan regretted what came next or not.

But for myself, I can say this: the Fox is many things. And exhausted, hollowed out, with only the fire of rage within them, they remembered that of all things they were, they were not a murderer. And they said to us, with a heartbreaking bittersweetness, that in that moment, they remembered the look in their kit's eyes on those precious few days they'd had together. The innocence, the brightness, the joy, the boundless love already present there...

For that lost child, they would not become what the Wolf deserved.

To this day, I can only marvel at the strength it took, maybe still takes, to honor that lost child instead of satisfying their own pain.

With the backing of their entire family, the Wolf was cast out, sent to crawl on his belly into the Wildwood of Zemin and stay there forever. A banishment that sundered the heavens and sent a god off on their own, blood of family forever staining his rotten soul.

Of the Fox after?

All T'sidaan said was they vowed to never let the Wolf hurt others, to stop him at the borders of every machination, every attempt for power and control. And, remembering the face of their child, vowed to never do so in a way that threatened who they were. To rise above evil while bringing evil low would indeed be a challenge. But one they vowed with their whole heart.

That vow came later, though, they said.

What followed after they let the Wolf live in shame is unknown. If the Fox did anything else after leaving the Wolf on that shore, no tale has ever recorded it, and

Audition for the Fox

T'sidaan stopped their own telling there. Attempts at mirth soon arrived after, and we all could tell: though they wished for us to know the truth of them, in that story they did not wish to linger. And who could blame them?

But . . . if I had to guess what followed, on my own and for no one but you, I bet they went home. Numbly opened the door of their now-empty little house in the Woods of the World. And seeing no one waiting for them, curled around themself like a flame burning itself low in grief, and mourned. I can only imagine they mourn still.

The moral of this story should be evident but let it be said: there are indeed ways to bring justice to the evil and wicked that does not destroy one's soul in the process. And for extra measure, let it not be said that gods do not mourn their children, that they would not go to the ends of the earth to protect those they love.

I still find myself haunted by what I saw as they finished speaking: tears of gold falling down their face, painting their fur bright.

They dripped down their face in slow, chaotic trails.

And to this day, I swear, it was as though T'sidaan's tears had been drawn by the loving hands of a child too young for a name but with a heart already so full of love.

—From the personal journal of Acolyte Nesi Indozo, recounting her time auditioning for the Fox; note: no recording of this tale into temple records

PART FIVE

THE SKULK IN WINTER

In the end, the trick was to tell the right story.

Since the Occupation began, when the gray-hulled ships of Zemin landed on the shores of Oranoya, the Wolfhounds had conquered more than a culture, more than a land; they had stolen the story of the Oranoyan people.

They had reduced it, hacking away at it with sword and screed, with shackles and cinders, made every Oranoyan go to sleep with this new story of who they were now ablaze in their minds, so bright it could burn away who they used to be, who they truly were.

Nesi knew she had to do more than open the doors of the fortress, more than break the chains holding back her people. For the last four months, she had chipped away at their efforts, but it would take more than one person to fight that kind of poison.

No, she knew now: she had to return the story of the Oranoyan back to them in a real and tangible way, give them the chance to write their own next chapter, not their conquerors.

She had to give them a tomorrow that belonged to them.

Impossible, maybe. Even for a god, or a champion with their favor, a daughter of Oranoya with a hunger for freedom or the son of conquerors, both of them eager to help.

But in the end, all it took was a handful of everyday favors, a quick note written on a napkin, a healthy diet of superstition, some overripe tomatoes, a common winter weed the Zeminis really should have plucked the moment they made this fortress their home, and yes, a morsel of illusion from a god of tricks, proud of their student and those she enlisted to their collective cause.

The Feast of the Wolf in Winter approached, and the fortress came alive with effort from all sides. Wood had to be gathered for the massive firepit. Hunting parties scoured the surrounding forest for elk and boar, whatever hadn't been slaughtered and salted already. Seamstresses toiled thread by thread as sashes were sewn, washers hauled laundry by the barrelful, and the cooks in the kitchens weathered the shouting of commanding officers who said, "all must be perfect!" even as those shouting could not tell you a teaspoon from a tablespoon, nor sugar from salt.

As the day approached, officers and guardsmen and the captive Oranoya each had a thought: where had the troublemaker Nesi gotten to? Rumors lived in the breathing space between people crushed together on the sewing line; they flew in the air between those in the fields, pulling vegetables before the ground froze over.

The old uncles said she'd finally been killed, buried somewhere nearby, shaking their heads at the pain that could've been so easily avoided, but how else did a story like theirs end?

The weathered aunties said she was hanging from a rope in an officer's house, abused and abased and now left for the crows and the cold, sighing at the waste of a life too bright to see common sense, but how else did a story like theirs end?

The ancient one who lived at the back of the C4 barrack, who would draw for you from the Deck of the Family of Stars when no guards were around, they said Ogre had done her in and devoured her in the dark, bones and all. But how else did a story like theirs end?

When they drew T'sidaan the Fox, a final reading for the dead, Una had to stifle a laugh and when the elder stared at her, she had to shake her head and said, "Don't worry, j'unse, inside joke." Then kissing their head, she ran out the barrack door, chuckling.

The ancient one said nothing, only contemplated the many meanings of the fire-bright tail dashing through the woodrot and why it showed up here, in their gnarled hand, at the height of the Wolf's celestial power.

Among all the Oranoya, a single young girl said that maybe Nesi had escaped! Climbed the walls, vaulted the spikes, and left down the snowy mountainside. Her and her compatriots, the other children in the fortress, thought this the ideal outcome. But all of them were shushed by their elders. Some, because they knew it was a fantasy, that no one escaped the Wolfhounds. Others, because the pain of knowing someone escaped and didn't take any of them with her . . . that hurt much more than anything.

But as had become the refrain: how else *did* a story like theirs end, anyway?

Over the two weeks it took for the Feast of the Wolf in Winter to arrive, no one saw that dark-haired young woman anymore, nor heard the ghost of her laughter, or her cries of pain. Even Ogre was strangely absent, spotted on the exterior walls on patrol, but without a mouse racing underfoot, it seemed he had no need to walk amongst his soldiers.

And so the work continued and the snow came and melted and arrived once more on the morning of the pageant.

Officers sat at a long wooden table in the cold courtyard, drinking their froth-brimmed dark ales like nothing could ever harm them. They savored crispy, tender boar and sweet potatoes thick with dark tamarind and plum sauce, disdainful of Oranoyan culture, but more than happy to eat their recipes, written in the hands of ancestors. The steam from the hot food shielded their gaze from the hundreds and hundreds of captives before them, mouths watering. Low-ranking officers each held a stone mug of meager ale, eyeing the nearly six hundred Oranoyan they'd brought to the yard. Forced to sit on the shivering stone, all of them watched Wolfhounds eat their food and love it like they could never love the spiceless bland shit they ate back in their city-forest.

The lead officers at the table had no care for their freezing, miserable audience. Didn't look twice as low-ranking officers went back to the barrels for more ale, and had no reason to check on the soldiers who lounged on the walls, bored.

They saw only the food, the drink, and of course, the performance.

For below the dais they were on, young men in the infantry, free of weapons and clad in costume, acted out a brand-new play from their homeland. *Topple The Sky, O Snarling Savior* was about the Emperor of the Hunt and Exiled Pillar, the Wolf, tearing down the Pillars of his sneering siblings, bringing equality even to the gods.

The captive Oranoyan shivered in the hundreds, ordered to watch their gods die.

Among them, a small red-headed figure crept, supported by a small woman with her hair pulled back, bangles removed, furtive and unnoticed in the crowd. They handed out something warm and soft. When the Oranoyan looked down at the fabric in their hands all of a sudden, away from the disgusting play, they felt a jolt in their heart.

But as one, they said nothing, sensing a shift in the wind. The two said to be ready, to let the officers eat. Let them drink.

The moment for action would come, but not yet.

As the play ended, the frozen ground littered with dead, toppled Pillars, a hush fell over the crowd. The far doors of the tower opened and out stepped the massive form of Ogre.

Behind him, he dragged a prone body; a young woman with long, dark hair, leaking red onto the snow and ice.

Many in the crowd gasped or swore or wept, as dozens of rumors collapsed into a single, cold truth.

Ogre took step after slow step until he reached the stage, dragging Nesi's body up the stairs; the hollow thunk of her body, step after step, was nauseating.

Finally, Ogre stood at the center of the table, forty high officers trembling to behold him. In silence, he threw Nesi's prone body to the stones, before the front line of Oranoyan elders. She did not move.

Then, he turned, handing a white piece of fabric to the officer on his left, pale-faced with fear, looking like a child in his dress clothes next to the Ogre.

The officer took it, staring into the horrifying helm above him. "You want that I should . . . read this?"

A single nod from the bloody wolf helm.

The officer nodded, sweat beading along his brow in the chilly air. He cleared his throat, blinked once, twice. He was having trouble focusing.

His voice stuttered through the air like a shaking bell.

"D-Did you know . . . that there is a certain compound in tuskweed that . . . every Oranoyan knows to avoid? It—it is harmless in s-small am-amounts but in l-large amounts, it c-could be . . . p-p-pretty bad. Good th-thing it doesn't t-taste like anything . . ."

Murmurs broke out around him, officers suddenly eyeing the food and drink with wild-eyed suspicion. A few at the other end of the table slapped hands to their foreheads, feeling for fever, looking each other in the eye. A few shouts from the infantry, pretending to be dead gods, wondering what was wrong.

Ogre shoved the man, pointed back at the napkin.

The officer looked up, vision now swimming, the wolf's face on the helm seeming alive, eager for his blood.

He wiped sweat out of his eyes, and spoke, the bell now cracked and hollow.

In a loud, warbling voice, he said, "A-and d-did you ever notice how . . . how there are way more of us, th-than there ever have been . . . of you?"

The officer looked up from the note on the napkin, fully under the effect of crushed tuskweed in his meal, making his head loll and his tongue numb.

Staring back were hundreds of Oranoyan, still and solemn.

All of them wore fox masks made of orange and black and white fabric.

The courtyard exploded with motion.

The table upended as each officer realized what was happening; their tongues went limp in their mouth. Their vision doubled, tripled. They knew the sweat dripping down their brow wasn't just spice but something far worse as they lost feeling in their fingers and toes, stumbling as numbness flooded in.

The infantry turned actors, out of armor and without weapons, began to panic. They threw away their drinks, their food, paranoia leaking into them as their commanding officers started to collapse.

It was then that a single, clear voice rang out, amplified by divine power.

Nesi got to her feet, reeking of tomato and soil. "You

see, this is what I *never* understood about the whole 'Lone Wolf this,' and 'Lonely Throne that,' of your precious Wolf. That is *not* the way to run together in a pack. I'd argue we could do better, right kyos? Let's show them how it's done!"

Nesi thrust a mask over her face and looked out through the eyeholes. With a barking laugh, a ghostly echo to T'sidaan's own, she leapt to her feet, jumped onstage and with her great-grandfather's strength shoved Ogre with all her might.

The empty armor, its enchantments from T'sidaan having served their purpose, broke apart and toppled all over the officer's table.

With a thunderous exclamation, the Ogre fell and shattered, the cage of it finally broken open.

It was that sound, like a story reclaimed, that announced freedom. The fox-masked captives of the fortress raced to claim it.

With a cacophony of shouting, yipping, and laughing, Oranoyan of all ages rose up like a tide of orange and black and white, rushing for their captors.

Nesi whooped and joined the skulk of them, this group of fleet-foxen freedom fighters ready to make this story their own again. With T'sidaan's voice in her mind, she kept low and to the shadows, as officer after officer began to panic, joining her skulk as they pushed their occupiers out.

She laughed as she became one fox among many, biting the ankles of their poisoned, weaponless occupiers and together, begin to drive them all out into the deep, lonely forest where wolves belonged.

Nesi stood with Teor and Una at the mouth of the fortress, their only light the pinion feather turned dagger, burning at their feet on the stone.

It had taken a few days of vigilance to keep the Wolfhounds from returning. But without their armor or weapons, all they could do was howl at the walls. And when the Oranoyan came out, brandishing those very things at them, they made themselves scarce, fleeing for good.

And now, it was quiet enough that you could hear a soul laughing on the other side of the fortress. Nesi never knew how loud violence could be until it was gone.

And in that peace and silence, everyone was finding a way to move on.

Many of the Oranoyan had kept their masks, vowing to slip into the town at the base of the mountain, and bring the Fox's justice everywhere a Wolfhound pissed against a wall and thought that made it theirs. Others sewed the masks into their dresses and scarves and robes and hoods, keeping the Fox close at hand as they made their way home, hoping to spread the word of T'sidaan and show it was possible to slip your shackles.

Others had stayed behind in the fortress, having nowhere to go and wanting nowhere to be. Nesi had hoped her friends would stay and find a future away from violence and war. But instead, they were here, about to leave. Teor with his silver cane (stolen from an officer's room) and Una with her signature grin and newly acquired winter robes, they each had a travel pack and lantern to guide them. Standing with them, a winter wind sending a chill down her spine, Nesi found a new fear hiding within her: that she could have won it all and still lost.

"You're sure?" she asked, knowing their answers; it was not the first time she had begged them to stay.

Teor nodded as Una glared with good humor at Nesi. "You can't keep us from the work to be done, Nesi," Teor said, his voice mild, his back bent and twisted. No matter the care he got, he would never properly heal from the torture his sister and the Spider had enforced on him. "But we know it's only because you care. We appreciate it."

Una sniffed, looking away with a grin. "Speak for yourself, poet. I don't appreciate someone trying to keep me out of the thick of it."

Nesi's heart broke staring at the two people she'd grown so close to while here in the past She wanted to scream, to grab their wrists and pull them back into the fortress, out of the jaw of history, salivating and eager.

The Occupation doesn't end for another thirty years.

The Occupation leads to the largest war this world has ever seen.

The war does what wars do and how do you outrun something whose shadow touches everything?

But she said none of these things. She took Teor's hand and then Una's, gripping them both to her chest, unable to stop the tears from falling. "I just don't want to see either of you get hurt. We've come so far."

Una squeezed her hand and kissed her brow. "Which means we still have so much further to go, kyo. Let us go change the world."

Teor pulled her hand to him, kissing the back of it. "You saved us, Nesi. Now we're going to go save others. I think it's the only way we can repay you properly. Freedom earned is only as good as freedom gifted, remember? We have to pass it on. Or at least try, or I owe a beautiful Hawk an explanation."

Nesi was crying, heart racing, trying to find a way out of this horror. History books flashed before her, paper specters haunting her. The books wanted to tell her what happened to her friends; their weight smothered her, insisted on what would be and could not be changed.

With all her might, Nesi forced herself to believe that their future was their own and *anything* could happen.

It filled her so overwhelmingly, a rush of understanding that if she had learned anything, it was that fate could be thrown aside; nothing was written that could not be erased. Any tomorrow could be chosen if you just fought hard enough. That's why she was sent here! Why work so hard in the first place if nothing could be changed?

She had to stay. She had to. These were her friends, her people! She'd finally found them and now they were going to leave.

No. Nesi could not let that happen.

Let her choose *this* tomorrow.

A sudden flame ignited within her and she said, "Let me help then! I—I'll go grab my pack. Just a minute more, please! Let's go together." She spun on her heel, unthinking, heedless of consequence but knowing in the depths of her soul, she was making the right decision.

Audition for the Fox

Before her, all of history stretched out. It was vast, unknowable! And Nesi saw all the time in the world to make things right. To figure it out. What she wanted, what she needed.

Nesi finally had a future of her own and she was racing for it with her arms wide.

She ran back to the barracks where her meager belongings waited, the door screaming on its hinges as she ran to the satchel on her cot.

Cinching the straps tight, Nesi felt a smile overtake her, delirious with the possibility before her.

Nesi didn't look back. Why would she? She wasn't leaving.

Before her, the door opened to the cold, dark quiet of a winter's night, her friends only feet away. As Nesi hoisted the bag on her back, she marched out into the night.

She stepped through the door.

Thump.

A hollow sound. Not snow. Not stone.

Dark wood?

Light, terrible and sudden, blared all around her.

The cold vanished; heat surrounded her. Her nose filled with the heady scent of thick, sweet incense.

Awful, familiar incense.

Nesi blinked, trying to see clearly. It took her a moment to understand where she was, to place the smattering of tallow, the reed mats on the floor, the wooden visages staring at her . . .

She . . .

Home.

She was home.

Nesi gaped like a fish gasping for air, heart hammering, a pressure in her chest rising. Snow drifted off her shoulders as she looked around. She . . . she couldn't breathe. Where was the door? She couldn't—couldn't breathe!

Teor and Una, they were waiting for her.

They were—they were in the past. No.

No, no, no, this wasn't happening!

Tears, sudden and hot. Her hands curled into fists, arms and legs shaking. She felt sick. The flash of three hundred years gone in an instant was going to—she was going to vomit. She couldn't breathe, she—

T'sidaan appeared in front of her.

That's right, some faraway part of her said. *The audition . . . it's over.*

Nesi was weeping and couldn't say if it was from joy or sorrow because had any of it even fucking mattered?

The question was in her red-rimmed eyes, full of tears, silently begging for the Fox to say something, anything. They looked at her from a remove with those haunting butterscotch eyes, their face haloed in golden candlelight. Their gaze was full and enigmatic, their shoulders tense and shaking, as though they wished they could say a thousand things, but only had the ability to utter a single phrase. Standing in their divine raiment, smelling of lavender and sage and ash, Nesi couldn't bear their terrible beauty and cold silence anymore.

"Tell me," she said, voice raw, body shaking, almost begging. "Tell me it was worth it. Please! Please tell me they don't die for nothing."

Audition for the Fox

The Fox cocked their head, as though a far-off animal had caught their ear. They had never seemed so otherworldly, so alien. Sighing in a voice like a gentle rain meeting a still pond, and they kneeled down to look her in the eye. A soft, warm hand came up to meet her cheek and their thumb gently smoothed the tears from her face.

They said, "Rest, Nesi. Rest. And yes. Sadly, it's always worth it."

Then, the Fox vanished as a familiar set of robes rushed toward her, then swallowed her in a hug.

She wept, a sound leaking from between her teeth, as Authoritative Ren kept saying, "Oh gods, oh gods, what happened? Nesi, what happened? Where did you go? Where did they take you? Nesi, talk to me, please!"

She cried for the pain she'd been dealt, the injury witnessed, the loss felt over and over. She cried for lives taken and lives freed. She cried for her new friends, going out into an uncertain world. She cried because she wasn't there.

Mostly she cried because, for a moment, she had forgotten all about the audition.

Nesi had counted the days, had tasted the hours as they passed by. She had been in that fortress prison for just shy of five months, give or take a revolution.

Authoritative Ren said she'd been gone for only a single hour.

Everything she'd been through crashed into her like a storm wall and Nesi wept like a woman out of time.

A TALE BETWEEN PILLARS

THE FOX AND THE TURTLE

IN THE DAYS BEFORE you and I were brought forth from clay and cloud, the Fox of Tricks owed a favor to the Turtle of Patience.

It is said the Turtle can watch a seed grow into the tallest pine without blinking, that he watches stone weather away for centuries with nothing but good humor. If there was a god to test his patience, it was the Fox, indebted to the Turtle for a good deed done in the previous century.

In his own plodding way, the Turtle finally cornered the Fox, remembering his sibling's debt.

The Fox had the decency to blush, bowing to their brother. "Brother Turtle," they said, "I am well and truly caught. Outdone by my own arrogance, thinking I could elude you forever."

A smile started to reach the corner of the Turtle's mouth, though it would take a month before it reached the corners of his wide mouth. "Nothing escapes me, younger sibling. From the wheeling of heavenly bodies to the bounding of your fleet feet, all come back to me in the end."

The Fox nodded, accepting the wisdom with nary a sarcastic word. "But of course, Brother Turtle. All things in their time, even my education. So, how might I repay this favor I owe you?"

The Turtle, whose siblings called him Golorth'ta, gestured to his shell, larger than mountains and tougher than diamond. "It has been some time since my shell has been cleaned and scrubbed. I ask that you take some cloth and make my shell shine like a pearl, sibling."

The Fox, whose siblings called them T'sidaan, held up their delicate, furred hands, nails shining black and fragile. "A mighty task! One I am not fit for, brother. For my hands are delicate things, all music, no muscle. And my nails, why, one wrong glance chips them in the most unflattering way. Alas, I think this task beyond me. And were I to even attempt such a feat, it would surely take me a decade to complete! How would you feel, unable to move for ten or more long, long years of my ceaseless chatter, for I shall have to entertain myself with all sorts of song and conversation!"

He would never admit it but even Golorth'ta, Turtle of Patience, had his limits. But much like his heavenly domain, to his detriment, he would not back down. "Why, my dedicants only need a year to wash my shell, T'sidaan. It would take you nearly ten times as long?"

Eyes downcast, they nodded and said, "Oh yes, brother. Maybe longer, for I am loathe to admit, but I have never been one for manual talents and I fear my lamentations will join the queue of my entertainment."

Silence, as Golorth'ta weighed the honor of a favor owed repaid against ten or more long years of T'sidaan's unending nonsense.

In that silence, T'sidaan smiled, for the Fox has always known when to pounce on prey.

They cleared their throat. "If such a situation were deemed unfavorable, brother, I . . . may have a solution. One that would benefit the both of us, perhaps?"

Golorth'ta looked up, secretly relieved. "Is that so, sibling? Tell us."

The Fox's smile was brighter than the crescent moon and twice as sharp. "I propose this! Let me shrink you, dear brother. To the span of my palm. It shall make cleaning your shell a simple thing and you will have to put up with my prattle for no more than an hour's time, maybe less if I focus! What say you?"

This made the Turtle pause. He was not the Pillar of Humility and so knew he was vain about his size, loving how his mighty shell looked against the curtain of the sky.

T'sidaan could sense his hesitation. "Oh, brother! I promise: soon as I'm done, you will be free of me. All debts repaid; I hope?"

Golorth'ta could already feel the satisfaction of having his favor repaid *and* saving himself a decade of his little sibling's complaining. "This is satisfactory. Work your magic, T'sidaan."

True to their word, the Fox uttered a syllable of woodsmoke and crow's caw, weaving the magic of acorns and wildflowers and other small things around their brother.

And in their hand hand, T'sidaan went to work, rubbing lavender soap into his jade shell, massaging dirt away, only telling a few handfuls of anecdotes which, Golorth'ta would admit later after his anger had faded, were mostly pleasant.

At the end of the hour, their brother's shell almost brilliant in its cleanliness, T'sidaan sighed. "I must admit, brother, this has been fun. I should owe you favors more often."

Golorth'ta, strangely, found himself melancholy that their time was nearly over. "It . . . has been enjoyable. Maybe we we could spend more time together, my sibling."

"Why not start now?" they said with a wicked little yip, stuffing their brother into a robe pocket far deeper and wider than any mortal garment.

The tiny Golorth'ta sputtered, squeaky and panicked. "B-but you said I would be free of you!"

"When I'm done! There is a small spot on the back of your shell that is just *not* as bright as I think it could be. So I still have work to do. But since it sounds like you've nowhere to be *and* wish to spend more time together, we may as well go and have some fun before I complete my debt!"

"T'sidaan!" the Turtle shouted, muffled inside the pocket, "I will have you hunted by my dedicants. I will have you skinned and put on a mantle!"

The Fox pouted as they skipped into the Woods of the World. "Not a very charitable way to begin our time together, brother! Well, all shall be made right; let's go find some fun!"

With a bark of laughter, the Fox of Tricks made for corners of the world where delight was to be found, a turtle in their pocket, screaming for release.

Golorth'ta stayed in their company for a total of nine years, seven months, six days and an hour, slightly shy of the task's original estimate of a decade. In that time, he had been skipped across twenty-one lakes, dashed against a multitude of rocks, spent three years in the gullet of a kraken, and used as a wager in a game of cards, (which his sibling promptly lost).

When his dedicants finally convinced T'sidaan to give their god back, they chuckled, handed him over, and vanished. Once free from his sibling's magic, Golorth'ta regrew to his original, mighty proportions with a fury to match.

For many years, it seemed the lesson was this: that between a fox's fortune and fury, many should make an enemy of them, for it seemed that being a trickster's friend was often more dangerous than being their foe.

Yet for all his anger, it was said Golorth'ta would lose himself in thought at times, his rage giving way to quiet contemplation. His dedicants would find him smiling when they thought his fury still lingered.

Finally, a young dedicant asked: why smile so, if you are still upset with your sibling? It took Golorth'ta a few years to find the answer, but when he spoke, it was with warmth.

"For all my sibling frustrates me, for all their chaos, I don't think I would've seen the world as I did without them. I would never have sought adventure as they did, never have tried my hand at cards or drank mortal concoctions or any number of things. Was it dangerous? Yes. But even when I was trapped in the kraken's gullet, they visited. There were many times we laughed in that belly together. And when the kraken surfaced, I tasted the salt-heavy air of the sea, and did you know? The stars look so different on the other side of the world. I didn't know that. But now, I do. Isn't that extraordinary?"

It was some years more before the Turtle let their sibling come and visit, but softened when they came with a gift of lavender soap. When asked by a dedicant about their decade together, T'sidaan only ever said they'd be happy to do so again, and that when you travel with a trickster, danger and delight often go hand in hand.

But, as we have come to know, the lesson is this: true harm never comes to those who are friends to the Fox.

> —Audio recorded at the Celebration of the Golden Moon, held at Old Dragon Palace in Qaffinu, one of several humorous tales told to honor Pillars of fortitude, harvest, joy, and summer

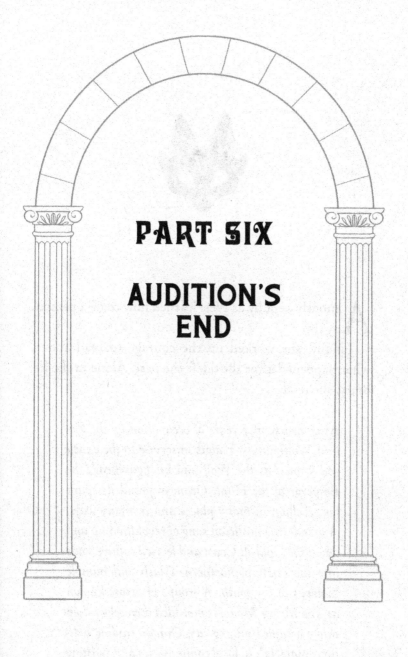

PART SIX

AUDITION'S END

A month went by as Nesi learned how to be a person again.

Finally, she worked up the courage to read about what happened after she'd left the past. Alone in the library, she read:

> After nearly fifty years of occupation by the Zemin Wolfhounds, zealots in service to the exiled god known as the Wolf and his figurehead, the Emperor of the Hunt, Oranoya found its spark for rebellion in many places and in many ways. A wandering musician sang of revolution up and down the Goldsilt Coast and ferried captive souls into the safety of northern Yylash and humble Nolorus to the south. A troupe of actors known as The Merry Makers embedded themselves deep in the occupied mining city, Oraqar, trading seditious materials to local communities and twisting

the plays of the Zeminis to deliver subtle messages of uprising.

And deep in the western mountains known as the Cloudbreakers, at a fortress responsible for an expansive timber trade, Wolfhounds were driven out en masse by a large group of Oranoyan, who came to call themselves the Kits, or Children of the Fox. Like a tide, these mischief makers and trouble starters went from town to town down the mountains, the valley, and into the country proper, using tricks, pranks, misdirection, and local knowledge of flora, fauna, and geography to free their fellow countrymen and inspire others to join them in their guerilla warfare.

By the end of Occupation, the Children of the Fox numbered in the tens of thousands. And though the widespread fervor for tricky T'sidaan waned as we entered the Age of Progress, many Oranoyan keep a candle for the Fox, ever eager to thank them and show their loyalty as a child might to a parent.

Nesi sat there, absorbing what she'd read. They'd been right. She hadn't been alone. And it had worked. It had really worked. It...

Across from her, T'sidaan appeared, their form emerging from a sudden cascade of autumn leaves. Nesi sat across from them in silence, staring, trying to make sure they were real before she spoke.

She wanted to ask them everything. But she satisfied herself with, "You left me alone. Why?"

To their credit, the Fox looked down at the table as they carved an intricate sigil with their sharp, dark nail. "You needed a clean break from the past. I am . . . not always the best at mortal emotions. If I'd stayed, I'd have done more harm than good."

She saw their point. Could only fathom their helplessness at watching Nesi flash back to the trauma she'd endured, imagine the half-hearted attempts to help her normalize to the present. They were right. They would have been useless and Nesi would've resented them, always looking for them to take her back or to fix her broken heart, which only time can stitch back together.

Then, "I was going to stay, you know. I had already decided, when you swooped in to take me." The look in their eye told her that they had known. "Is that why you took me away so fast?" Reflecting on it now, staying was a decision that almost certainly would've gotten her killed.

T'sidaan's voice was soft with understanding. "We help stories, Nesi. We nudge, we correct, we push when need be. But we are not a part of any story but our own. The story moves on without us and if we stayed to see how it ended, well . . . we'd leave our own stories behind."

"You'd never have let me stay anyway, would you?" Nesi had come to terms with it, had mourned for Teor and Una, for those goodbyes that would only ever live in her heart and not theirs. But they were right. The story yearns to end and cannot; Nesi would've ended up sacrificing her life to see it through.

"No, I would not have. First, it would've created quite

the paradox if you'd died in the past before you could travel back there in the first place. Not one I couldn't fix but, that's beside the point. Second, I'd be a little miffed if you ran away into the past right when I was about to extend you a job offer."

Nesi's heart leapt into her throat. She felt it beating just under her tongue. Her mouth went dry with fear and joy as she said, "You're . . . wait, you're serious?"

A solemn nod, even as a joyous light arrived in their eyes. "I am. I'm here to officially become your divine chaperone, with you as my sole acolyte, Nesi, if you'll have me."

Nesi stammered as heat rose to her face. "But why? I . . . I wept! I panicked, I got beaten, I couldn't handle it. T'sidaan, I nearly ran away into the damn past, I—!"

T'sidaan raised their hand and Nesi wouldn't dare speak through that brilliant light in their eye, like the sun seen through a pinhole.

"You, Nesi, have nothing to be ashamed about. Yes, you may have lost your place in the story here and there, but you never lost your purpose. When faced with insurmountable odds, tyrants to throw down, in a time that was not your own, with only your wits, charisma, and yes, heart, you saw your audition through until the very end. You not only threw down the wicked, you did so by lifting up the brightness of those around you. Because of you, your country was able to start reclaiming its story, its future. You took to my realm of trickery with little prodding and any guidance you needed was only to keep you from despair, not entice you to hope. *That* you had in abundance. I think," they said, with their telltale smirk, "there is much good we can do together and many more joys that exist tomorrow than do today."

Nesi felt herself looking into her own past, saw it splinter like a prism, each moment of failure only a single facet that she had had to see through to get to where she was.

Here, a god that found her and her heart worthy.

She had done it. She had proven herself.

"Oh. Wow. I mean, thank you, but . . . yeah, no, I'm good. Thanks, though."

An orange eyebrow shot up as the other plummeted down, eyes flaring molten as T'sidaan stood, knocking over their chair. "*Excuse* me?"

Nesi burst out laughing, shaking from sheer giddines. "I'm kidding! I'm just kidding! I couldn't resist, I'm so sorry, please don't take back your offer. I would be honored to be your acolyte, T'sidaan."

The god crossed their arms and sniffed. "Well! You have much to learn still, pup. Firstly, the difference between a trick and a joke, which you're still not very good at . . . yet."

"I suppose you have your work cut out for you, then," Nesi said, relief washing over her, mingling with adrenaline. She looked around the library, already saying goodbye. Saw a lonely mountain temple she'd never have to live in.

She was free. She was free! And knew: tomorrow had so many stories to tell her.

"I suppose she said yes?"

Turning, Nesi saw Authoritative Ren standing with a backpack in his hand, his face beaming even as tears stained his holy raiment. "The Fox paid me a visit. They let me know their intent, and I figured if you said yes, you might need some provisions, your things, a few snacks, maybe a paperback or two—"

Nesi barreled into him, wrapping her arms around him. His arms enclosed her as he whispered into her ear, "I never had any doubts, my friend. I'm so proud of you."

All she might say fell away before the two words that would mean anything. "Thank you," she said, "Thank you for believing in me."

Passing the bag into her hands, Authoritative Ren smiled and said, "I'd say be careful, but I think it's everyone else who needs to be on the lookout. The mischief you two will get up to!" Looking to T'sidaan, he said, "My Pillar, please bring her and visit once in a while. I should like to hear of your adventures together. And do please keep her safe."

With unexpected reverence, the Fox bowed before Authoritative Ren, saying, "Though danger and delight often go hand in hand where I walk, I will do my best to make sure she experiences the latter more than the former. My thanks, Authoritative. I'll light a candle for the good work you've done shepherding these students, especially Nesi."

It was rare to see him blush, and yet, Authoritative Ren's cheeks grew crimson at the thought of a Pillar lighting a candle. And for him! His bow was so deep, his nose nearly touched the library floor. "I'd be honored, great Fox. Thank you. May your days to come be filled with comfort and light." With that, he gave Nesi one last hug and said, "And I hope to see you soon, Nesi. Bring good stories to me?"

"Only if you bring good wine," she said, grinning and returning the embrace before stepping away toward T'sidaan.

Laughing, Authoritative Ren finally wiped the tears from his eyes. "I had a feeling you'd say something like that. I'll do my best." With that, he smiled, nodded, and left the library, taking Nesi's past with him.

Shouldering her pack, a question occurred to Nesi. "Before we go," she said, "what happened to Teor? To Una? Did they . . .?"

The Fox gifted her a rare full smile, warm and sincere. "They traveled together for a little while, brought together by certain strings of fate," they said, pointing at Nesi. "Two years in, Una was wounded in a small town called Ozhon. She survived, but it ended her nomadic lifestyle. She made a life with the printer's daughter, falling in love over seditious flyers and decent political cartoons. No children, but if you go to the bookstore in Ozhon, there is a little plaque with her and her wife's name on it, speaking of the good they did. They are remembered.

"As for Teor, he stole away on a ship, back to Kehora. He never saw his family again, but I'm happy to say he did go on to become a truly middling poet. No major awards, but his work advocating for unity, respect for all, and a Zemini future that did not stain its history books with blood was well-received. He was quoted often by the new Zemin Unilateral Parliament, his words a yoke that bent new leaders toward more noble ideals.

Turns out his most lauded collection was dedicated to my feathered sister, but his first collection, often called, 'his most passable,' was dedicated to me, which I find endlessly delightful," they said, chuckling. "A good life, I think, one free of cages. He never married but he was content with a life of words, work, and friendship. And he was remembered."

"They lived on," Nesi murmured, "remembered by time itself."

"If it makes you feel better, Teor's father died mad," T'sidaan said. "Nothing like living forever to piss off a terrible father and family. *Especially* through middling poetry."

Nesi nodded, trying to understand that bittersweet feeling deep in her heart. History had not eaten her friends. They had escaped those jaws and lived lives worth their weight in gold. Smiling even as her eyes grew misty, Nesi said, "Thank you, T'sidaan. Seriously, thank you."

They bowed from the waist, deeper than Nesi had any right to. "You deserved to know. And I'm glad for it. We do what we do for many reasons, but sole among them is that so all children of clay and cloud may lead lives of worth, love, dignity, and respect. And if we're very lucky, there will even be some good stories along the way.

"And speaking of stories to be told," they said, offering their hand, "there's a little town near the southland rivers of Oranoya that's going to need help dealing with a riddle-loving salt dragon in about, oh, ninety years. Apparently, she's quite cross for a reason she won't tell anyone who can't match wits with her. Want to see how fast we can ruffle those crusty scales of hers for some answers?"

Nesi saw all of space and time bloom open for her, a garden she knew she'd tend as long as she could, rescuing and preserving the stories of everyone, everywhere.

She took their hand, smiled, and said, "It would be my honor, T'sidaan."

With a bark of laughter, Nesi and the Fox vanished into tomorrow, leaving the library smelling of lemons and woodsmoke, both eager to see what stories they could find together and save.

AFTERWORD

Where and when are the Fox and Nesi off to in time? Well, maybe someday we'll find out what happens with that particular salt dragon, how the Fox really feels about cellphones (intense dislike), and more across the vast width and breadth of our world of Pillars and mortals.

If you've come this far, thank you so much for reading. The Fox would be the first to tell you that attention is truly the dearer currency we mortals can spend in our lives, especially in this day and age; that you chose to spend that coin on my story with Nesi and the Fox is truly special, and on behalf of my characters as well as myself, thank you for being here.

This novella had a long and strange road to become what it is, which makes sense, given the general chaos within. What was a five thousand-word conversation between Nesi and T'sidaan in 2019 became a very long short story, and then a much longer novelette, and while

I grumbled for a while about just how long this short story thought it was going to get, and then my friend, editor Brent Lambert said, "Got anything novella-shaped?" and the story said nothing but I swear I could feel T'sidaan's toothy little smile through the laptop screen, the cheeky trickster.

But I don't regret that road for a moment. Some stories need time to grow and blossom, and *Audition for the Fox* took the time it needed. Much has happened in those ensuing years, and I've grown , too. Hell, I'm married! I'm an uncle three times over! I've started taking walks at six in the morning. Wow. A lot *has* happened.

Some things remain the same though. I still think we need tricksters to tweak the nose of tyrants. I still think we need loving, inclusive, intersectional communities that can hold space for all those who lack such a thing, and embrace them in that held space and into community. I still think there will always be a part of me that feels like Nesi: too young, too inexperienced, too anxious while also wildly passionate, eager to help, and desperate to fulfill a purpose. And I still think stories are some of the best tools we have in the world to save each other, through joy, shared experience, human connection, and the healing power of art.

Man, I really hope I get to do this again. Publish a book, I mean. I really couldn't tell you what comes next, but I'll keep my fingers crossed it happens. Normally that kind of uncertainty would throw me for quite the loop. But as Nesi learns, sometimes you just need to act, whether you're ready or not. Sometimes, you build your own tomorrow, and if you're lucky and work hard and remember to chuckle once in a while, you can even get there.

So, I can promise this. I'm going to keep writing and telling stories. I'm going to do my best to move through this world with empathy, compassion, joy, and laughter. And anytime I see a fox, you can bet I'm going to thank T'sidaan for their blessing, their wit, their huge heart, and their patience as I wrote this first story with them and Nesi.

I promise, if there's a next time, I'll give the two of them a nice, swanky ballroom scene, a big, modern kind of bash with tiny teacakes and fancy cocktails and expensive outfits and politicking and courtship drama, real *Bridgerton* vibes. Yeah . . . something tells me they'd both enjoy that, maybe too much.

Something tells me there may just be a story there . . .

Martin Cahill
2025, New York

ACKNOWLEDGEMENTS

I'VE BEEN IN THIS BUSINESS way too long to take anything for granted or believe another book is a guarantee. And I've also been alive too long to believe that gratitude of any kind should be measured out in trickles and drops. What does that mean for you, dear reader? Buckle in. This is going to be a long one.

I would not have made it this far had I not the encouragement, support, and kindness of many teachers, professors, and mentors, some of whom have become dear friends. From Sacred Heart School, thank you to Mrs. Ulmer, Mrs. Fox, and Mrs. Olsen; from Albertus Magnus High School, thank you to Rose Ruppino, Mary Rivers, Greg Mower, and Nate Mello; from my teen years, thank you to Marc Buxton, Kris Dougherty, and the late, great Denny O'Neil; from college, thank you to Jill Hanifan, James Farrell, Dr. Lisa B. Thompson, Langdon Brown, Ronald Bosco, Yvonne Perry, and Paul Ricciardi; from Clarion, thank you to Greg Frost,

Geoff Ryman, Catherynne Valente, N. K. Jemisin, Ann VanderMeer, and Jeff VanderMeer; and a special thank you to Kat Howard and Joey Haeck. Each and every one of you incredible educators, mentors, friends, and writers gave, and still give me, the gift of your time, brilliance, kindness, and support, and I can never thank you all enough, (though you know me, I'll still try). Thank you each for believing in me, teaching me, and cheering me on, always.

I must also thank those in my life who learned with me, stood by me, and added their voices to the cheering crowd that I know is there, even when my worst days try to have me hear silence. To my fellow Clarion students of 2014, you have my love and thanks for challenging me as a writer, embracing me as a friend, and for being rocks of support ever since. To the members of my writing group, Altered Fluid, thank you for taking me in after Clarion, and providing week after week of critique, community, and showcasing the joy of the work itself, of writing. For the last chunk of my life, Erewhon Books has been my home. To my talented colleagues, thank you not just for being some of the best in the business, but also for your incredible friendships as we weathered storm after storm. And a sincere thanks, many years due, for my college comedy club, The Sketchy Characters; never was there more fertile ground to plant oneself in and grow, to be given space to play and laugh and make becoming an adult just a little more hilarious and memorable. Thank you each for four years of sweet lunacy and for helping me become funny enough not to have made this book a totally humorless slog of a read.

A mighty thank you to those editors and writers who've championed my short fiction and other creative works; I'm so grateful that each of you saw something in my work worth sharing with the world. Thank you, Brian White, John Joseph Adams, Wendy Wagner, Scott Andrews, E. Catherine Tobler, Daniel José Older, Carmen Maria Machado, Marco Palmieri, Yanni Kuznia, Aigner Loren Wilson, Neil Clarke, Jonathan Strahan, Ann VanderMeer, Fran Wilde and Julian Yap, Sadie Lowry, Sarah Peed, and Richard Thomas. And to all those first readers and editors who rejected my stories and sent words of encouragement, thank you, because that kindness means so much and I know keeps the fire alive in the hearts of many a writer; it did for me, and still does.

To dear, dear friends of mine, from many chapters of my life, my sincere thanks for always having my back, for pushing me, supporting me, and helping me tell stories. To Jesse, Mar, Kelsea, Lauren M., Amanda, and Bella, to Matt and Erica, Tess, Paul, Nick, Matt G. and Liat, Sammy and Chris, Mike, Katie, Christine, and Lauren B., to Manish, Nino, Nibs, Em, James, Hillary, Danielle, Megan, Maggie, Trevor, Kyle, and Elisha, to Cass, Viengsamai, Diana, Kasie, and Sarah, to John Wiswell, Alexandra Rowland, Eric Smith, Ola Hill, Bradley Englert, Lyndsie Manusos, Claire Cooney and Carlos Hernandez, Ali Trotta, Cass Khaw, and Lisa Rodgers, I am so, so grateful for each and every one of you. If friendship were gold, I'd be rich beyond compare.

My sincere thanks to my beta readers for this story, whose many thoughts, joys, grumbles, and laughs helped guide this novella into its final form. Naseem, Victor,

Danielle, and Pearse, T'sidaan, Nesi, and I owe you much; thank you so much for walking through these woods with us. In addition, I cannot stress enough how much of an impact Brent Lambert had on this novella; he saw this story grow through nearly every iteration, and never stopped believing in it or in me, and helped me see it through to the end. Nothing but gratitude, my friend; let's keep telling stories together.

To Team Tachyon, my utmost and sincere gratitude for welcoming this goofball into your fold. To Jaymee, I can never thank you enough for loving this story as I do, and for using your incredible eye to make it as strong and silly as possible. To Kasey, your depth of talent is second only to your incandescent kindness; thank you for your hard work and dedication, and without you, this book would have had to make a home in the dark. Thank you both for bringing this novella into the light, and thank you to the whole team for making such a beautiful dream made real in my hands.

To my blurbers, thank you for taking the time to read Nesi's journey and for your help in telling people about it. At the time of writing this, there are no blurbs present, but I'm going to be optimistic, pre-grateful one could say, that they're all so amazing and meaningful and kind, and that we actually had to turn away authors, famous ones, seriously, Mr. King, please, next time, I swear, you're on the top of the list! But seriously, if I even get one blurb, it could even be lukewarm, I'll be grateful beyond imagining.

To Hannah Bowman, nothing but my immense gratitude as you've helped shepherd me through this process, and for your constant encouragement whenever worry or panic strikes. T'sidaan brought us together, and I know they're wishing us luck as we continue to walk down this road of stories together.

To my mom and my dad, thank you both for putting books in my hands and stories in my heart; I needed them. Thank you both for only gently insisting I not read at the dinner table while everyone was still eating, and even then, only really enforcing it at holidays. Thank you both for teaching me how to tell stories, how to speak and move and engage with others. And with utmost sincerity, thank you mom and dad for never once saying that my dreams of becoming a full-time writer were silly, only that if I were to make a go at it, to please have a job that paid some amount of money and to try not to live at home into my forties, (if I could help it, shit happens). I wouldn't have made it this far without you both loving me and my big heart and my hunger for stories, as much as you could. I love you both so much, always. Thank you both, always.

To my brothers, Brendan and Mike, thank you both for listening to me ramble about story ideas, especially when I was first starting to write. They probably weren't very great, sorry, but you were good sports about it. And as I grew up, and got somewhat better at the aforementioned ramble, you both have been nothing but supportive and insistent I go out there and do the damn thing. Thank you, brothers. And to Staci, Hudson, and Nora, to Ilana and Micha, thank you all for being a part of our family and becoming my family; each of you are such a gift and my life is richer with you all in it.

To my wife, Cosette, you have my eternal gratitude and my entire heart, that place where my love for you burns bright within me and always will. You are my wife, my partner, my best friend, and my number one fan. I am crying writing this right now (you know it's true). I have never met someone who so completes me in every way imaginable. By the Pillars, I am so lucky. Thank you for always cheering me on, lifting me up on bad days, celebrating my wins, reminding me to advocate for myself, and being an absolute goofball with me. I hesitate to even write down any of our bits lest readers believe us to be mad. But it's our kind of madness. I love you so much, Cosette, always. Here's to you. Here's to me. Here's to us, and wherever our story goes next.

A final thank you, once again to you, dear reader. Thank you for walking with Nesi and the Fox for a spell. I hope you enjoyed your time with them, maybe even enough to tell a friend or two. But I deeply hope someday, if I'm lucky enough, you'll come on back for whatever story I tell next.

BOOK CLUB QUESTIONS

1. The reader is dropped into the story right along with Nesi, each having to figure out where they are and why. How do you see the author working to give clues to each party? How does the author balance bringing readers into the narrative in medias res with worldbuilding?

2. Nesi's struggle is fairly universal, outside the divine involvement. Do you think she makes the right choice with the Fox, or should she have waited? What would you have done?

3. From her praying to the Fox, we learn much of Nesi's struggle through her many failures with the other Pillars. How does the author help the reader understand Nesi's mental-health struggles, and what does the reader glean from her impulsiveness?

4. This story includes magic as well as science fiction concepts, such as the Bootstrap Paradox.

How do you feel about the overlapping genres? What do they tell you about this world and these characters?

5. The Fox is a trickster, a being known for direct action, but so often they move in the shadows with Nesi. Why do you think this is? What is the author saying about tricksters with the Fox's indirect action?

6. So much of the history between Oranoya and Zemin is directly related to the relationships among the Pillars. How do you see one reflecting the other? And do you think the health of these nations can affect the gods?

7. Teor provides our first perspective from within Zemin that is not authoritarian, and we see how he has been forced to be a captive himself. How does Teor's time in the armor mirror the captivity of the Oranoyan? How do their struggles echo each other's or differ from one another's?

8. In the end, Nesi does not rely on violence to ignite the revolution. In your interpretation, what were the key elements to her success? And were they things she learned from the Fox or already knew as an acolyte?

9. Nesi almost stays in the past, confident she will be staying with Teor and Una. Do you think the Fox is right to take her home? And what do you think would have happened if she'd stayed?

10. Stories play an important role throughout the book, and throughout we see many different perspectives on the Fox especially. Do you believe the Fox is a character that is known by the end? Or do you believe there is still mystery to them?

11. Did you have a favorite Pillar? Who and why?

12. Of the themes running through this text, what do you believe is the strongest one and why? How do you think the author balanced each component?

MARTIN CAHILL is a writer living just outside of New York City and works in his day job for Erewhon Books, an imprint of Kensington that publishes science fiction, fantasy, horror, and everything in between. His short story "Godmeat," appeared in *The Best American Science Fiction & Fantasy 2019* and his story, "The Fifth Horseman," was nominated for the 2022 Ignyte Award for Best Short Story.

A graduate of the 2014 Clarion Writers Workshop, Martin has published many pieces of short fiction across a variety of venues. Those venues include *Fireside Magazine, Reactor, Clarkesworld, Lightspeed Magazine, Beneath Ceaseless Skies, Shimmer Magazine, Nightmare*

Magazine, and *Sunday Morning Transport*. He was one of the writers on *Batman: The Blind Cut* from Realm Media. Martin has also written game material for Ghostfire Gaming, D&D Adventurer, and Darrington Press.

Martin also writes, and has written, book reviews, articles, and essays for *Reactor, D&D Adventurer, Catapult, Ghostfire Gaming, Book Riot, Strange Horizons*, and the Barnes & Noble Science Fiction & Fantasy Blog. He also published an essay chapbook with Calque Press entitled *This Map Is Yours or How Videogames, Their Forms, and Their Art Saved Me*. He's thrilled to debut with this novella from the excellent folks at Tachyon Publications.